Getting **OUT** *of Town*

Getting OUT of Town

CONNIE BARNES ROSE

Copyright © Connie Barnes Rose, 1997

All rights reserved. The use of any part of this publication, reproduced, transmitted in any form or by any means, electronic, mechanical, photocopying, recording, or otherwise, or stored in a retrieval system, without the prior written consent of the publisher — or, in case of photocopying or other reprographic copying, a licence from Canadian Reprography Collective — is an infringement of the copyright law.

The publisher gratefully acknowledges the support of the Canada Council, the Ontario Arts Council, and the Department of Canadian Heritage.

The author wishes to thank Terry Byrnes whose encouragement and advice helped immeasurably in bringing this book into being.

The stories and characters depicted in this book are fictional and are not intended to represent any actual person or event.

Earlier versions of some of the stories have been published previously. "Knights" was published in *Fiddlehead*, "The Scrag and the Chess Set" in *Matrix*, "Action Avenue" on the internet in *It's a Bunny*, "Escaping Escape" in *Blood and Aphorisms* and in *Scribner's Best of the Fiction Workshops 1997* (Simon & Schuster, Inc.)

Edited by Gena K. Gorrell.

Printed and bound in Canada.

Cormorant Books Inc.
RR 1, Dunvegan, Ontario
Canada K0C 1J0

Canadian Cataloguing in Publication Data
Rose, Connie Barnes, 1954-
Getting out of town
ISBN 1-896951-03-1
I. Title.
PS85 85.O72544G47 1997   C813'.54   C97-900389-X
PR9199.3.R5878G47 1997

*This book is dedicated
with love and appreciation
to
Anna T. and Marlene D.
and
especially to my parents*

CONTENTS

ESCAPING ESCAPE 1
ACTION AVENUE 17
KNIGHTS 27
UP UNDER THE SUBWAY 39
RIGHT INTO THE SCREAMERS 49
GETTING OUT OF TOWN 61
THE SCRAG AND THE CHESS SET 107
BECAUSE OF THE TIME CHANGE 121

ESCAPING ESCAPE

The man I love has just walked into the visiting-room. His hands are stuck in his pockets, his bald head shines under all the bright lights. You'd think he was wandering down the street by the way he looks around at the inmates sitting there, each with a number stamped on his breast pocket. Most of them sit across from women who stare into their eyes and hold their hands tightly across tabletops. Finally he stops at my table and, sitting down across from me, stares at the window.

"You've shaved it off again," I say, trying to catch his eyes.

I wish I hadn't said that. He ignores me when I say things that aren't all that important. I fiddle with a piece of gum wrapper that someone has left on the table, and wait for Tyler to come out of his meditation. Tyler can meditate anywhere. He has told me meditation is one of the two things that help him survive in here. The other is the excellent hashish.

Now he stands up. He raises his arms high above his head. "It feels so good to stretch," he finally says, smiling down at me. "It makes me feel like a cat."

I say, "I know what you mean. I've been doing a lot of yoga lately."

GETTING OUT OF TOWN

"That's good, Natasha. Yoga will keep you in touch with yourself." Then he laughs. "You know what I find funny?" He jerks his thumb back towards the guards in the observation booth behind him. "Them. They think they have me locked up in here when I'm as free in here as I am anywhere. They're the ones in prison. Look at them there."

I look at the guards, knowing exactly what he means. They're there every time I come here, which is at least twice a week. They sit in the same chairs, wear the same uniform, and don't look one bit freer than the men who live here all the time.

"Look at the fat one," says Tyler. "Is he looking this way?"

I look at the fat one. He's reading a newspaper. The other guard is watching an inmate who stretches his arm across the table to stroke his girlfriend's hair. "It's okay," I say.

Tyler reaches down and slips his fingers into the side of his running shoe. Then he folds his hands in front of him and nods to the paper cup on the table. "Pass it over when it's clear."

I slide the empty cup over and he slips a rolled-up wad of money into it. I quickly look over at the guards before I pull the cup back to my side of the table. He smiles at me as I take out the roll and slip it down the front of my jeans.

"Ah, Natasha," he says. "It's good to see you."

Tyler likes to call me Natasha, even though my name is just Nancy. The summer before last, we ran into each other on the beach, out on the hard red flats. It must have been fate that brought us there on such a windy, cloudy day. He had just come out of prison after catching a five-year sentence for selling a couple of joints to some stupid university kid who got caught and got scared. Before he was put away, I'd only known Tyler from seeing him hanging around town. With his green leather jacket and long red hair, he reminded me of Robin Hood. But out there on the flats I thought he just looked alone. We walked along the sand-bars and he wanted to know all about the music I liked, whether I turned on, if I had ever tried to meditate.

Back on the shore, my father watched us from the cottage we were renting for the week. My father is a town cop. The first time Tyler got busted, he said, "I'm glad they got him before he went and ruined some kid's life." I was only fifteen then but I remember thinking that what my father said sounded pretty weird, seeing as Tyler was the one who was going to prison. So I guess it shouldn't have surprised me that he wouldn't be too happy to see me out on the flats with Tyler when he'd just been paroled. I reminded him that there wasn't much he could do about it, seeing as I was now eighteen. He told me that as long as I was living under his roof, I wasn't allowed to see Tyler King.

The next night I met Tyler in a field. He spread out a blanket and we lay on our backs and just paid attention to the universe. After we smoked a joint, he pulled a timothy straw from its shaft and began to stroke my forehead with its fuzzy tip. He told me about the seven chakras contained within our bodies. Slowly he dragged the straw down over my chin, my shirt, and my bare skin below it, stopping at each chakra to explain what it meant. Then he ran the straw down the zipper of my jeans to right between my legs. You'd think, with all that denim separating me from a straw, that I wouldn't feel a thing, but when he stroked me with it I just about went nuts.

"Now, we think of this as the lowliest of all the chakras," he said, smiling at me as I lay there trying not to squirm or laugh or cry, "but you see how powerful it can be?"

Until that night, the only guys I'd kissed had tasted like beer. That night I fell in love with Tyler with all my heart.

GETTING OUT OF TOWN

The visiting-room is getting pretty noisy with all the laughing and talking, and kids running around the tables. Tyler takes my hand. "Have any of the seeds come yet?"

"Not yet," I say, "but I only ordered them last week."

"How are they sending them?" he asks as he twists the little silver ring on my finger.

"By bus," I say.

"That's what I thought."

We have a big garden out behind the apartment we rent in town. A couple of weeks ago I brought in some organic seed catalogues and Tyler and I had the best time planning this year's garden. I even brought in some Crayola markers and we drew a blueprint. We got a little carried away with actually colouring in the corn and tomatoes, but it was fun. The guards kept coming over to see it, and shaking their heads. Tyler liked the picture so much he tacked it up in his cell. He won't be able to work in the garden this year since he's stuck in here, but he'll be out by harvest time and I think, by planning it with me, he can see an end to all this.

I say, "I figure, as soon as this month is over, I'll borrow a rototiller. That is, if the snow ever leaves." My words trail off. I've lost him again. He stares at something on the floor.

Tyler landed back in here because he broke his parole last September. He was out at the beach with Helmer McKay, checking out Helm's cannabis crop. The RCMP didn't actually catch him with the plants but they turned down the road into the field just as Tyler and Helm were leaving it. Ty's parole officer said he couldn't buy the story that he'd only gone down that lane for a swim. So for that he's back in for at least a year, even if they couldn't prove anything, and look at Helm still strutting around town. "That's how the system works," Ty said to me the first time I went in to see him. "Once they get you, they got you for good. What if I'd just been down there for a picnic?"

When I reminded him that he'd broken his parole conditions just by hanging around with Helmer, who everybody knows is a dealer, he stood up, all pissed off, and said, "You're missing the point, Natasha. They don't want to see me free because they think I'm a threat to the whole of society. You should know how these people operate by now."

I couldn't believe he was getting so pissed at this. He stood up and I grabbed his arm.

"I can't be with someone who thinks the way *they* do," he said, walking away. Through the door, I saw him raise his arms to be frisked. He looked up at the ceiling as the guard ran his hands lightly along his sleeves. When the door shut him from my view, I stood there stunned for a minute before I could move. I cried all the way back to town. Maybe he couldn't escape from those prison walls, but he sure could escape from me.

When I got back to town, I drove straight to Alana and Danny's. Alana was hanging out a wash in the backyard. Even in winter she hangs out her wash. She says seeing it flapping in the wind makes her feel safe somehow. After she made us some tea, we went out on the back steps. "That Tyler," she said, "is chock full of shit." Alana has known Tyler all her life. She says that she loves him like a brother but that I should know by now he works things to suit his own ideas of how life should be. "But I understand how he must feel," she says, twisting her hair up into a bun. "I know I'd go nuts being locked up in there and knowing everybody else was running around free."

Maybe Alana knew him before, but I think that's what makes her blind to what he's really about, what *we* are about. Tyler and I are not like ordinary people who are controlled by primitive emotions. We don't even use the word "love" except when we're talking about all of humanity.

GETTING OUT OF TOWN

A lot of Tyler's old friends laugh at him behind his back. They knew him from before, when he was just like everybody else. They don't know how much he changed in prison. I'm the only one who believes him when he says that all he really wants to do is buy some land in the country where we can grow our own food and live quiet lives. I believe him because that's what is most honest about him. He wants to feel free in this world. And I do too.

I can understand why Alana and Danny are a little pissed at him, though. Not long before he got sent back in, Tyler decided we should only breathe clean air, and since Danny or Alana weren't about to stop smoking cigarettes, we would have to stop going there. "Besides, they eat meat. Can't you smell it on them?" I couldn't, and I sure didn't want to stop seeing Alana, but Tyler was right about one thing. If I was going to try to live a healthier life, I should avoid temptation. Before I met Tyler I did stuff like smoke cigarettes and eat hot dogs. Tyler says that one day we won't want to smoke cannabis any more either. But for now it's okay because of the way it sweeps the dirt out of the far corners of the mind.

Now Tyler raises his eyes to meet mine. He says, "Have you seen Jack lately?"

"Yesterday," I say. Jack is Tyler's cousin. He's one of the people who like to laugh at Tyler, especially behind his back. Everybody calls him Father Jack because he has a job cleaning all the churches. And also because he jokes about being celibate seeing as his wife won't sleep with him, won't even talk to him half the time. He jokes around a lot, doing impressions of people around town. I have to admit he does a good one of Tyler. He closes his eyes and says something like "Ommm. We are one with the universe. To achieve divine perfection we must cleanse our minds and bodies. We must drop our possessions and clothes and live as nature intended."

ESCAPING ESCAPE

Then Jack will open one eye and say, "Nancy, or, pardon me, Natasha, you may start by removing all of your clothes. Then you may sit yourself down upon my holiness so that I may explore your inner self."

Jack told me he heard through the family that Tyler got raped soon after he went into prison that first time. "Tyler may have been fucked up before he went in, but that really fucked him fuckin' permanently," he said, not long after Tyler and I rented the apartment down on Deacon Street. Jack was there helping me clean it up while Tyler was at work at the big farm out by the beach. His job was driving a big liquid-manure spreader over the fields all day. He said he took the job because humility is the way towards truth.

I asked Tyler about the rape once. He just shook his head and said, "All of prison is rape, Natasha." But then he told me something that made prison not sound so bad. He said he met this inmate called Joss who was doing ten for sailing up the Fundy with hashish in his hull. He taught Tyler how to play chess and he gave him all these books to read. Tyler said that, after meeting Joss, he began to put his faith in fate.

"Give Jack a message," Tyler is telling me. "Tell him to throw the next bag over the fence behind the toolshed. Somebody on yard duty will pick it up. And this is important," he says, leaning closer. "Don't forget to tell him to make sure the bag matches the ground. Like if there's snow that day, put it in a white bag, but if there isn't, make it brown, okay?"

"Okay," I sigh. "But I thought you said you weren't going to be doing this any more."

Tyler nods. "It was supposed to be the last one, but Natasha, the way I see it, we're providing hope. This way they get to escape, at least for a little while. And it's a hell of a lot better than booze. I wish you could see how peaceful it is in here since I've been back. Even the screws are starting to wonder."

"That's what I'm afraid of."

"What can they do, throw me in prison?" He puts his hands up to his face, looking at me over the tips of his fingers. "It takes courage to live like us, Natasha, whether we're taking risks, or just surviving. We've chosen a path that goes beyond ordinary life. At least I have. Sometimes I'm not so sure you're ready."

"I have to go to the bathroom," I say, because I can see in his eyes that he has shut me out like I'm no different from one of the screws over there. I go into the visitors' washroom and lock the door. I run water in the sink and splash my face. I look at myself in the mirror. I have a very red pimple on the side of my nose.

I remember another time I was in this washroom, looking in this mirror. I'd gotten up from the table and slipped in here to wait for Tyler to follow me in. As soon as he'd slid around the door, he locked it and turned me so I was facing the sink. He pulled my long skirt up around my waist. I held onto the sink and stared at my face in the faucet chrome. It was all bent out of shape, my nose swollen to three times its size, my lips looking twice as wide. I almost laughed, until I looked up at myself in the mirror over the sink and saw that I really looked fucking scared. But it was exciting scared too, the way we hurried, all the danger we were in. After, Tyler smoothed down my skirt and kissed my neck and I walked out of there calm as any summer day. Tyler came out soon after, and nodded to the inmate mopping the floor near the washroom door. After we sat down we couldn't stop laughing. The guards were looking at us, and every time we looked up at them we'd start laughing all over again.

When I come back from splashing my face, I half expect Tyler to be gone. But he's still there, sitting with his eyes closed, his head swaying just a little, as if he's listening to music. When I sit down he says, "I'm sorry, Natasha." I'm wondering what he means by that, like if he's going to jump up any second and walk out again. I touch his sleeve and say, "Ty?"

"Life is full of contradictions" is all he says, just before he opens his eyes. Sometimes I think he can read my mind.

A bell rings at the end of visiting hour. Chairs scrape and the guards come out of their booths to make sure nobody gets carried away in their goodbyes. Sometimes when I'm carrying the money I worry about spot checks. But like Tyler says, it's not illegal to carry money.

Tyler holds me close, nuzzling his face into my hair "Sometimes I think you're the strongest person I know," he says, then pulls away and marches quickly to the door, leaving me standing there as usual, wondering what he meant.

Today the guards are in a good mood, and they joke with us as we sign out. They don't even bother to check any of our bags.

"See you ladies next week," says one, winking at his friend.

"And don't you worry," says the other. "The boys will still be right here when you come back."

The last sliding gate rattles shut behind me. I gulp at the cold air blowing up from the bay. I feel the eyes of the guard up in the tower as I walk to my car. Behind the wheel, my knees start shaking so much I can hardly keep my foot on the pedal.

I guess you could say I'm a prison widow. Alana told me I couldn't be luckier. "Look," she said, "here you get to be single and free, but you know you've got someone a short drive away who's jerking off just for you. When they're loose, who the hell knows what they're up to?" Maybe she needs a break from Danny. They've been together since they were seventeen. He drinks too much but, then again, she doesn't put up with much shit. He hit her once, slapped her face because she called him an asshole. But she just picked up a breadboard and slammed him so hard that we got a little worried later on when he started mumbling about being on some carnival ride. Maybe he is an asshole when he drinks, but when he's sober he and Alana sometimes disappear for hours and then come back hanging off each other, like it had been their very first time.

It was hard getting used to Tyler being gone at first. Mostly I was just lonely. We'd shut ourselves off from the people in this town, and it got so we could pretend no one else existed when we walked through the streets in our long navy coats. There's no furniture in our apartment except for a mattress and a long oriental rug that Tyler got from his grandmother when she died. On that carpet we read and meditated. We practised our yoga and tai chi. The room was so long that I could do running handsprings. Sometimes I could hardly wait for him to leave the room so I could go flying through the air, then sit down again before he came back. "What was all that noise?" he'd say, and I'd say a truck must have driven by or something. I don't know why I didn't want to do them around him. I guess I was worried he'd think I was being childish.

Jack is at the Jupiter Restaurant, sitting in his usual booth, the second from the door. He asks me how Tyler is. "Bald," I say, and then wish I hadn't.

Jack laughs into his coffee. "I bet he's a pretty sight. The great guru. When are you going to shave your hair off, Nance?"

I hand him the money. He counts it. "I'd say he did well with the last stuff, wouldn't you?"

"I have no idea," I say. "I just want him to stop doing it."

ESCAPING ESCAPE

"I thought you wanted this land-in-the-country thing too," he says, stuffing the money into his pocket. "I keep telling him we should be bringing in fucking cocaine. A kilo of that would speed things up real quick."

"I have to go," I say, getting up.

"Oh, by the way, Nance," he says, and for some reason the way he says it makes me stop in my tracks. "There's a package coming in on the bus tomorrow and it has your name on it."

I sit back down. I know he doesn't mean any organic vegetable seeds. "What do you mean, my name?"

The waitress brings Jack his dinner. She puts it down and says, "Here you go, Father Jack. Oh, hi Nancy, I haven't seen you in a while."

I know her. We used to jig geometry class and go smoke in the washroom. I'd draw stuff all over the walls while she wrote things like 'Ruth McNair has no hair, underneath her underwear'. I remember that all right, but not her name.

"Can't complain," she says, heading back to the kitchen. "Enjoy your dinner, Father."

Jack watches her until she's gone through the door. He whispers, "Just what I said. You'd better pick it up, because I don't think it should sit around in the terminal too long, if you know what I mean."

I watch him dump ketchup on the burger. I watch him take a bite, then wipe the grease off his chin.

He says, "It's two pounds of hash, and it should be here by Monday."

Danny's getting drunk and cooking up some deer steaks he's pulled out of the freezer. The whole kitchen is full of gamy smoke. I'm sitting at the table playing crazy-eights with little Kevin.

Danny says, "Hey, Nance. You can go tell Tyler that we

had a totally natural dinner here. Yessiree, we've got your wild deer, and wild mushrooms, and lookee here, we've got your home-brewed beer too." He spears one of the steaks out of the frying-pan and, bringing it over to me, holds it under my nose. It smells like blood. I turn my head but all of a sudden I've got these juices flowing into my mouth.

"Come on, little Nancy, I won't tell," he says, trying to follow my nose with the steak.

Alana walks into the kitchen waving her hand at all the smoke, and saves me by asking if I want to go for a walk. She throws on Danny's hunting jacket and we start out along the old marsh road. It's quiet and dark here on the salt marshes. The road is a bit muddy yet so we have to step carefully. When we're far enough out of town and the stars are easier to see, Alana lights a joint. As soon as we get off, she gets to talking about her UFOs again. Ever since they found one of those rings out here, she's been right into watching the sky. I went and saw the ring, everybody in town did. It was perfect how it crushed the tall grass so it lay like dominoes, all splayed out from the circle. I walked around that circle, right in the rut. It felt pretty weird to think something might have been there. Most everybody says it was caused by a wind twist, but Alana's sure that, whatever it was, it'll be coming back.

She stands with her face tipped up to the sky and her hair riding down her back. I start thinking about the package that'll be riding the highway over this marsh on Monday with my name stuck on it. There's no way around it. I have to pick it up. I start pacing along the grassy ridge rising up in the middle of the road. The more I pace, the more I feel like screaming. I want to shout at whoever's up there, or out there or inside here, that maybe it's true I'm too weak, maybe I do want a regular old life. I don't know anything except one thing. I sure don't want to go to prison just to prove that I am free.

ESCAPING ESCAPE

Here I am, pacing faster and faster, turning and circling. I guess a noise must be coming out of my throat because suddenly Alana plants her hands hard on my shoulders. "What's wrong with you?" she says, her eyes wide open and looking all around as if maybe something has actually landed somewhere near. I sniff, look up at the sky, and wipe my eyes. "Alana, do you think Tyler really loves me?"

I shiver there in the dark. I can tell that Alana is frowning. "You mean you put up with all his shit and you don't even know if he loves you?"

My knees are knocking together like crazy. Maybe I'm being paranoid but, when I called to see if the bus had come in, the guy on the phone sounded kind of tense. For all I know, the narcs could be hiding somewhere in the building right now, just waiting for me to pick up that parcel.

I walk into the Terminal Diner. My father sometimes comes here for lunch with some of the other town cops, but he's not at his usual spot where the counter snakes around by the window. He likes to keep an eye out for things going on around town. Except I notice that, whenever I happen to walk by the window, his back is turned.

None of the other cops are here either, which really spooks me. Somebody waves to me from across the room and I wave back. It's just my old history teacher, who took a liking to me for some reason, and tried to talk me out of quitting school. I walk into the bus terminal. The waiting-room is empty too. I go straight past the ticket counter and into the women's washroom. I sit on a toilet and try to meditate. I close my eyes and concentrate on my mantra, listening to it until I know I'm locked in there where my eyes have trouble opening, where my head feels light and heavy too. For fifteen minutes I sit, until I start to feel like I've slept. I try to take a deep breath but the place stinks too much.

I open the door and, calm as can be, march right up to the booth. "Is there a package for me? Nancy McKinnon?"

The guy looks through a bunch of packages. "No-o," he says slowly as he sorts through them, "I don't think so...."

"Or maybe it's Natasha McKinnon?" I say, standing on tiptoes trying to read the packages.

"Oh, wait a sec, here it is, Nancy McKinnon, that you?"

"That's me," I say, smiling at him as sweetly as I can.

"Heavy for such a small package," he says as he passes it over. "Must be gold, is it?"

"Must be," I say, and I walk right out the door towards the United church.

Jack's down in the basement, arranging the same little chairs I used to sit on in Sunday school. He opens his mouth when I throw the package at him. But I'm out of there before he gets a chance to say a single word.

I'm back in the visiting-room. Tyler looks surprised when he comes through the door because this is not my usual visiting day.

"What's wrong?" he says.

"What's wrong is the package on the bus. The one that wasn't seeds."

Tyler leans back in his chair and folds his arms. "So? Did anything happen?"

"No," I say. "I was lucky."

Tyler smiles. "Ah, you see? Nothing happened. You really should have more faith in your own fate, Natasha."

I stare at Tyler. He stares back, his eyes calm and patient.

"My own fate?" I say, my voice cracking. I tap my fingers on the table and tell myself I *will not* cry.

"That wasn't my idea, to send it by bus," he says and shrugs, "but I knew you'd be safe. You're Leftie McKinnon's daughter. Nobody's going to touch you."

ESCAPING ESCAPE

There's a kind of buzz in my ears. He starts going on about strength and weakness and who has it and who doesn't. Alana and Danny don't have strength, they're just the same as everybody else. Jack doesn't, he was too chicken to go up to Toronto to pick it up himself, and that's because he's scared of any city bigger than Moncton. But me, he knows I have courage. I let him go on and on. I think about the last night we were together before he went back inside. He fell asleep before I did, and I saw how his closed lashes rested so lightly on his face. I couldn't stand to think of someone so beautiful being locked up in a cage.

"It's only through suffering that one realizes one has nothing left to lose, Natasha," he says. "This is a basic truth."

"Tyler," I say, clearing the catch in my throat, "my name is Nancy."

He sits back in his chair and shakes his head ever so slightly. "They got to you, didn't they?" he says. His green eyes watch me calmly, the eyes that made me believe.

ACTION AVENUE

I'm sitting on Bailey's bike and listening for the sound of Father Jack's old sportscar. I could have sworn I heard it gunning up under the subway, but now it sounds like it's down by the marsh. Wow, Carla must be flying that thing, because she seems to be somewhere up by the cemetery by now.

It's Thursday night and most people are sleeping, just waiting for their alarm clocks to scare the dreams right out of them. I hope Carla has the good sense not to buzz down past my father's house. He went off duty at eight, so I know he's not patrolling the streets tonight. Which is about the only reason I can tear through town on Bailey's ten-speed shouting, "Action Avenue!" instead of slinking around the sidestreets. Just thinking about this makes me raise my fists to the sky, and when the wind from behind picks up my jacket like a sail, it whisks me even faster down Main Street.

Main Street has that red glow it gets on summer nights. I guess this comes from the sandstone buildings. Or maybe it's the drugs. There are a few guys perched over on the park bench, high on magic mushrooms and wearing these funny little pixie grins. When I stop the bike next to them, Nick, the only one I know, says, "Hey Nancy, this stuff is really good."

"Ain't it though?" I say and wheel away. Bailey's tires hum on the pavement, my whole body is in rhythm with these legs that are as strong and tireless as the pistons on the train that's just now charging through town. I bike down to the tracks and stop so close to the train that the force of the wind blows my hair straight back from my face. As soon as the last car passes, there is this suction that lasts only for a second, but just in that second I feel like I'm about to get yanked right on after it. Then it's gone, the screaming steel noise, and right after the train has rattled away it gets quiet so suddenly that I can hear the nighthawks screeching.

Oh, and I can hear Carla again too. She's somewhere up by the cement works by the sounds of it. She's been getting pretty close to Father Jack these days. Not that I think they're doing it, Carla told me she doesn't like him that way at all. What she does like is anything to do with speed.

Bailey has gotten himself into speed in a big way too. He and Carla and Jack shoot up in the attic of the rooming-house Jack owns. It's been going on ever since Bailey moved in there. I knew at the time it probably wasn't too healthy for him to live at Jack's, but he wanted to get out from under his mother's roof and, since I'm still living in my father's house because no-fucking-body believes in tipping at the Jupiter, where I work, I told him I thought it was a good plan. But the simple truth was, I wanted a place where we could screw.

Bailey is two whole years younger than me. But he was so cute I couldn't keep my hands off him. Carla teased me when she saw I had a thing for him, said things like "You sure he's allowed out after dark?" He was almost eighteen, for Christ's sake, so I hardly think it was cradle-robbing. And besides, he's the one who started following me around town. I'd be at work at the Jupiter Restaurant, and he'd come in and order a piece of banana cream pie and then go on about how good it was. As if it was me who'd made it. I couldn't help noticing how he smoothed the hairs on his brown arms resting there on the counter. And he had these clear green eyes flecked with little dots of gold.

One night he showed up at the Purple Hall. I watched him go straight to the bar and ask Dennis for a beer. I saw Dennis fold his arms and ask Bailey for some ID. My heart went right out to him when he looked my way before walking out the door. And I just followed him right on out of there. Behind me I could hear Carla and the rest laughing. When I caught up to him at the bottom of the stairs, all I had to do was put my hand on his shoulder.

We got it on behind the Purple Hall, where a grassy bank runs down to the tracks. It was dark and I hustled him out of his clothes so quick that later he said he felt as if he'd been caught in a twister or something. When the Halifax train came through I decided we'd best roll behind a bush. That Bailey may have been young, but he didn't lose me for a second.

The sportscar comes screeching to a stop smack in front of me. My back wheel swings around and I just about bash into the door. Father Jack takes off this dotted red scarf he has wrapped around his eyes.

"I couldn't stare death in the eye any more," he says, wiping at his forehead.

Carla is so excited she looks like she's about to come. I once heard her say that the only thing that went with speed was more speed. And Jack with his car made the perfect match. If there's something to be had, you can be sure the Father has it. And like he says, he's always happy to share the magic with his friends. He also has this thing for bows and arrows. There's a line of tin pie plates stuck on the barn behind his rooming-house. At any time of the day or night you can hear the arrows rip through them. It used to amaze me how Jack's tenants would put up with all the noise, until I figured out that they were mostly old drunks with nowhere else to go.

One day Bailey gave me a lesson in archery, because I was getting bored with smoking dope and screwing to Seals and Crofts. I liked how I felt, pulling the arrow back just as far as it could go. And I liked the way Bailey felt behind me, too, as he helped me guide the shaft along the bow. But mostly I liked how Bailey looked standing there with his long brown hair and steady gaze. So we soon ended up back on his mattress.

Father Jack asks me where Bailey is as he wraps the scarf around his neck, carefully tucking the ends in.

"He's at Chase's," I say. "There's a poker game or something going on over there."

"Go tell him something for me, will you?"

"Why can't you?" I say, because I like to think I've developed a thing for not doing what I'm told.

Jack throws his hands up. "You'd think I was asking her to rob a bank. He's your boyfriend, for Christ's sake."

Carla has moved herself up so she's sitting on the back of the seat. She has lit a cigarette and looks like she's not noticing this conversation. But of course she is.

"Why don't you say please?" she says. "Bailey may be your butler, but Nancy isn't."

That's another thing that pisses me off about Bailey moving into the Father's. Instead of making Bailey pay rent, Jack has decided to call him his butler. He's supposed to take care of the house, clean the bathrooms, shovel snow, things like that. Bailey thinks he's getting a great deal here. When I complained to Carla about it, though, she said, "Maybe it's you who doesn't like being the butler's wife."

"Oh yeah," I said, "and what does that make you, Jack's

wife? Don't be so stupid, like I'd want to be anybody's wife."
I was pissed off at her the whole day.

Chase's poolroom looks all dark and I'm thinking maybe nobody's in there. I go and try the door and find it open. I start through the hall, because I see there's a bit of light coming from the back. I've never been in Chase's poolroom, because girls just don't go in there. I suppose that in itself might be a good reason to start, but the truth is, I never wanted to before, and I don't really want to go now only I have this message from Jack. It has to do with the stash, it has to be moved tonight. I'd do it myself, but it's under Jack's barn and I'm afraid of skunks. For sure Father Jack isn't about to crawl under there, and since Bailey is the butler, well, it's his job. When I pointed out that fetching Bailey wasn't *my* job, Jack told me he wasn't about to go into Chase's poolroom himself. Carla and I tried to get him to tell us why, but all we got was that he didn't feel like dealing with Ricky Chase tonight and, if I would be so kind, could I deliver the fucking message to Bailey about moving the stash. I didn't let on but I knew what it was, the thing with him and Ricky Chase. One night last winter I came out of the Purple Hall and saw Jack pushing the girl he was living with up against a car. He was real mad at her and she was crying. Ricky Chase was walking by and told Jack to lay off. Jack told Ricky to mind his own fuckin' business, but I saw Ricky take Jack by the arm and say something real quiet to him. Jack just stormed off up the street, and his girl went after him. I tried to think of what Ricky could have said to Jack to make him back off like that. Ricky's a lot smaller than Father Jack.

    I don't really know Ricky Chase, since he's way older, but he seems to know me. Whenever I pass him in the street he smiles and says, "Hi, Nancy McKinnon." But then he walks on like it doesn't matter if I answer or not. Once I turned around to look at him after he'd passed and I got all embarrassed because he had turned around too. He just waved and kept on going, but for the rest of the day my face got all hot whenever I thought about it.

The ceiling of Chase's poolroom droops down like a hammock. The lights dangle low over the tables. At the end of the poolroom a light shines from a room. I call out, "Hey, is Bailey in there?"

I hear the scrape of a chair and Ricky Chase comes out of the room. He's wearing a white shirt that just about glows in the dark. He turns on the lights and I stand there blinking.

"Oh, I thought Bailey would be here. He said there was a poker game."

"Why, it's Nancy McKinnon."

"So is there a poker game?" I say, wondering why I feel so out of breath.

He runs his hand through his hair as if he's very tired. "No, no poker game tonight, just going over the books for this place. Hey, are you any good at math? Come and take a look at this."

I open my mouth to say no, but he has turned and gone back into what turns out to be an office. There's a filing cabinet and a table full of papers. A bottle of rye sits next to a dusty adding machine. He picks up the bottle and asks me if I want some. I hate whisky, but I take a sip anyway. Then he tells me he's just inherited the poolroom from his grandfather. He looks up at the ceiling and mutters that he guesses his grandfather must have hated him.

I say, "At least it's all yours now."

"So it is," he laughs, raising his glass. "All mine."

That's when I notice these drawings of faces pinned up on the walls. I recognize some of them. One is of this guy around town named Garby who everybody says is half monkey. I've seen him come out of Chase's, and head straight for the garbage cans by the door. I go to say something about the drawing, how much it actually looks like Garby, but then I'm a bit shocked to see right next to it a drawing of my father when he was younger, in his uniform. For some reason that gives me a shiver, the kind you get when someone walks on your grave.

"I have to go find Bailey," I say, "and I really am no good at math."

"That makes two of us." He sighs, rolling his shirtsleeves up over his elbows.

It feels cooler out on the street. In fact, I'm starting to shake. And I'm feeling grubby, a sure sign that something's wearing off. That Bailey. One morning I went looking for him at a house where there'd been a party the night before. Whoever let me in told me he was upstairs. I went up there and looked into one of the rooms. This girl Rena Dickson was lying asleep with her mouth open in a snore. Beside her was this buddy I'd never seen before. I was about to turn away when I noticed a pair of feet on the other side of Rena's head. I looked down at the end of the bed and there was Bailey, sound asleep, with his hair falling over his cheek. One of Rena's orange-painted toes was practically stuck in his ear. I just stood there with my arms crossed tightly and said, "Well, this is cute."

Later Bailey said that Jack had laid some heavy downers on them, and that he didn't even remember getting upstairs, let alone what he could have been doing lying naked in a bed with Rena Dickson and that buddy. As if that would make it okay. And then he said that he thought maybe it was time he started looking for a job, that there was an opening down at the metal plant. Maybe we could get our own place, like an apartment, and then have some kids. Life could be normal, he said, just before I picked up the chair I'd been sitting on and threw it at him. I stayed mad at him for a week, until one Friday night when I was walking down Main Street and he dropped to his knees in front of me and practically the whole town. I tried to move around him but he blocked my way. So I took him back. But not once did I tell him that I couldn't really see us ever living together.

Now I'm really starting to shake, probably from thinking about all that. I need something to calm me down. I listen for the sound of the sportscar. Jack would have something on him, Valium, hash, anything to take the edge off this shit. That's the only problem I have with the heavier stuff. It leaves you feeling raw. Yeah, some hashish would round off the night. And I still haven't found Bailey to give him the Father's message. I wouldn't mind curling up in those arms right now.

The sportscar is parked beside the rooming-house. I see that the blind has been pulled down on the kitchen window. I'm just going around to the back door when a cop car pulls into the driveway. It's not like I can run, they've got me in the headlights. A cop and a narc get out. I recognize the cop. He and my father sometimes go fishing.

A bust is already happening in the kitchen. I stand in the doorway with the cops behind me. Bailey is there, his face all calm, his hands folded in his lap, a smile at the corners of his mouth when he sees me. Carla sits at the chrome table playing with the salt and pepper shakers. Father Jack is hunched over in a chair, holding his head in his hands. He raises his head and looks pretty freaked out. One of the cops is holding the stash. No fucking wonder the Father is freaked. For a second I try to picture him in jail, but I just can't see him being anywhere but here around town.

One of the cops is writing something on a clipboard.

ACTION AVENUE

The one who fishes with my father still hasn't recognized me. I figure any second they're going to ask my name. Then Bailey stands up and they put cuffs on his hands.

"What's going on?" I say. "That's not your stuff, Bailey."

"Then whose do you suppose it is?" the cop with the clipboard says, his yellow teeth grinning at me.

I look quickly at Jack, but he's still staring pretty hard at the floor. My own teeth clamp shut.

Then I guess I must be standing there stunned or something, because I just watch Bailey walk right out of the kitchen. Through the window I see them put him into the car. He raises his cuffs to me, and I get this hot pain in my throat.

"We're through here," says the cop with the clipboard.

"Aren't you Leftie McKinnon's girl?" the cop who fishes with my father says. "Now, I don't think you really belong here, do you?"

I'm sitting on the steps in front of the Baptist church. It's starting to get light. Soon my father will wake up and clear out of the house, and at the station he'll hear all about last night. I wonder if any of them will have the nerve to tell him his daughter was involved. I wonder if he'll go over to the jail to speak to Bailey. My father has never taken Bailey too seriously. At least, he never seems to have anything much to say about him. When I first started staying out all night, he just asked me, "What loser is it this time?" Then when he saw me and Bailey down in front of the Manpower office one day he actually stopped. He was in uniform and he asked me if I was going to introduce him to my new friend. Bailey started to turn all green when I went right ahead and acted like we were at a garden party or something. My father shook his hand and told him he'd known his mother in high school, and to say hello to her. Bailey stumbled over the four words he managed to spit out, and kept flicking the hair out of his eyes. After that my father had this little laugh he used whenever I mentioned Bailey's name. One day he actually stopped me in the street and said right out of the blue, "I'm just curious. What is it you're trying to prove, anyway?"

Poor Bailey. I'm staring at the dirt on the sidewalk and wondering what it will be like visiting him in prison. He probably thinks he needs me more now than ever. What he really needs is a girl who's ready to settle him down. What he really needs is a girl who doesn't feel so empty.

I should go home. I don't have a watch on but there's that sun coming up over the town hall just like it's supposed to, and there's a robin chirping away as if it has everything to be cheerful about. I hear some singing, and I'm thinking somebody's up awful bright and early. Then I see him come around the corner of Pearl's Pharmacy and almost stumble against a parking meter.

"Hey, Nancy McKinnon," Ricky Chase calls to me, like it's quite okay to be sitting in the Baptist church doorway at six in the morning. "Keeping out of trouble?"

"Doing my best," I call out. "Hey, how'd you do with the books?"

"Just like you. Doing my best."

I watch him open the door beside the Jupiter Restaurant. Just before he closes it, he turns and waves to me. Here I've been waiting tables all this time, and I never knew that Ricky Chase was living right above my head.

KNIGHTS

Alana and I sit on tree stumps and talk about Danny. He's been on a drunk since Friday. Now it's Monday and Alana is sure he'll lose his job.

"He was passed out on the bathroom floor this morning. And the kids saw him, of course," she says, shaking her head.

I mostly listen and munch on my sandwich. When Alana's mad at Danny, it's best to let her go on about it.

"He makes me sick." She grabs at the end of her braid and flicks it in front of her face. I crunch up my tinfoil and stuff it into my knapsack. The blackflies are back, now that the breeze has dropped. I'm not looking forward to the afternoon. Already my back is sore and I'm feeling stickier than a June bug. I take my glasses off to clean them but then I put them right back on.

"Am I seeing things?" I say, and point down the hill to the logging road. A new and shiny car bumps and scrapes over the ruts. "Now who the hell...?"

Alana shields her eyes. "I don't know but, whoever it is, he must hate his car."

A man gets out of the car and Harold, our foreman, goes over to him. We watch them talking until the flies get to us.

"I guess that's our excitement for the day," says Alana and she buckles her tree tray to her waist. We pick up our planting guns and tramp over to our lines. Side by side we plug tiny spruce trees into the ground.

"I have to get away from him, Nancy," Alana says, stopping to unjam her gun. I lean on mine to wait for her. She wipes her face with her sleeve and looks at me. "You don't believe I'll do it, do you?"

I say, "Well, it's not like I haven't heard it before."

She starts planting again and picks up the pace. I hurry to keep up with her. It's easy to tell when she's mad because she works like there's a storm coming on and the hay's not in.

"The kids were too young before," she says. "I couldn't handle it."

"So how would you handle it now?"

"I just will, okay?" With that she jabs her gun hard into the ground, loads it, and whacks the tree into place.

A voice from behind us calls, "Hey, are you trying to plant that thing or bury it?"

We turn around to see Harold and the guy from the car puffing away from climbing up the hill. So we stop and stare.

"This here's Charles and he's down from Toronto," Harold says. "He's going to be hanging around for a week or so."

Charles reaches to shake our hands. I take off my glove to shake the softest hand I've ever felt on a man. Sweaty, too, so when he turns to Alana I wipe my hand on my jeans.

"Call me Chuck, okay?" he says, and laughs. "It seems to go better out here in the woods."

"Sure, Chuck." Alana laughs too, and I notice she doesn't wipe her hand.

Harold says, "I told Chuck here that you two are the

best planters we got."

Chuck tells us he's come to do some research on reforestation operations, and he wants to experience every aspect of our work.

"Could I try that thing?" he says, pointing to Alana's gun, and she hands it to him. He tries to poke it into the earth, but hits a rock instead. He pulls it up and jabs it harder. By the third try the blackflies have found their mark. The gun topples over as he slaps at his neck.

He picks it up and grins. "You guys must be pretty strong to do this all day."

"We're pretty tough, all right," Alana says. "Crazy too, right, Nancy?"

"Broke too," I say, but no one hears me.

Chuck hands the gun back to Alana and makes a big deal about how he'll likely need her help showing him how to do stuff. Then he nods at me and leaves.

We watch them walk away.

"So what do you think of our Chuck?" Alana says.

"Just another slicker, I'd say."

"Oh yeah? Quite the looker, I'd say."

"Really? You think he looks better than Danny?"

"I guess you haven't seen him lately, either that or you're blind," Alana says.

She plugs her gun back into the ground real hard and I wish I hadn't mentioned his name. If she goes any faster I'll collapse. I try to change the subject.

"How's Kim's eczema?" I ask.

"Better," she calls back. "That new cream helped."

Alana's the one who's the looker. Back in school, local businesses were always wanting to sponsor her in the Blueberry Queen Pageant. She would turn them down in her sweet way and later say, "Can you see me as a prize cow for Crowley's

Roofing and Siding? What a joke."

Danny's beautiful too. The first time Alana and I saw him was one Friday while she was staying with me and he was delivering oil to my father's house. He looked up from his nozzle and saw us watching from the window. I backed away shrieking, but Alana froze. I could have passed my hand right in front of her face and I think the two of them would have held that contact. Finally the oil overflowed and with a grin he was gone. Soon after that they met at a Curling Club dance. Then Alana got pregnant and they bought the trailer.

I'm not so beautiful but I am loyal. The first time Alana left him, Danny got real drunk. He talked me into going out to Rambler's Beach, where there was a party going on. There, near a bonfire at high tide, he said he wanted to screw me. I said no, but then I went home and cried.

The sun is pretty high when I return to camp. We tally up the trees we've planted and gather around. Chuck gives a little speech about how important he thinks our work is and how we'll one day show our grandchildren the forest we've created. I nudge Alana.

"That's if they don't cut it down first."

She smiles and I snicker, but I realize it's him she's smiling at. He has just finished his talk with a little joke about us having to be tough to do the job and a little crazy too. Everybody claps, then we all pile into the covered box on the back of the half-ton.

On the trip back to the highway we laugh and joke as the truck jostles us about. Chuck has jumped into his car and is following us. Alana sits by the back door and keeps turning her head to laugh in his direction. Only it looks as if she's laughing into space.

Alana and I are walking along the road to her trailer. She has invited me to supper. Along the way she's been whistling a tune, but the closer we get, the more it becomes a whisper.

"I bet he's still drunk."

"Two dollars says he isn't," I say. "He doesn't usually last this long."

"I never keep track," she says, and sighs. "His drunks just blur together."

She slings her bush jacket over her arm and stops to pick a daisy from the side of the road. She carefully pulls at its petals.

"Who is that for?" I say.

"Who do you think?" she says, and throws it away.

We turn down her lane. Down by the trailer, we see Danny carrying a bucket to the pony beside the barn. He pats its neck while it drinks. Kim and Kevin play on a rusty swing set nearby. By the back door there's a barbecue with something cooking on it.

I hold out my hand. "Two bucks, Lan."

The kids run up to us and Alana lays her arms on their shoulders as we reach the yard.

"Hi Danny," I say.

"I made some hamburgers," he says to Alana, "and I opened a can of spaghetti."

Danny doesn't look so good. His hair is dirty and sort of stuck together. Red blotches cover his face and he smells like the service station.

"Do you still have your job?" Alana asks with her hands on her hips.

"Sure," he mutters, "I made it in okay."

"Well, it's a friggin' wonder," she says, and stomps to the trailer door.

Danny's hand is shaking as he flips the burgers so I touch his shoulder and say, "Why don't you go take a shower?"

At supper Alana ignores Danny and just talks to me. She wants me to go with her tomorrow night to the Purple Hall because it's Ladies' Night. She's wondering what to do about a sitter.

"I'll be here," Danny says.

"You're not going?" I say.

"No way. If I was to go there I might drink, and if I drink Alana's going to throw me out, right, darlin'?" He slides his hand across the table to touch Alana's elbow, but she yanks it right away.

"You know, if you screw up on this job, we lose the trailer," she says quietly, and when he shrugs she slams her fork down and shouts, "Everything we have gets flushed down the toilet!"

She gets up and starts to bang things around in the sink. Danny looks down and I keep eating. The kids chatter to each other. They're pretending that their noodles are worms. I guess Danny's stomach is a little tender, because he gets up and leaves the trailer in a hurry. I go to help Alana clean up, but since she's still as grouchy as a wet cat I say I'm going home.

Outside, Danny is lying on the hood of his car, his back against the windshield. I lean against the fender and light a smoke.

"Nice night," I say.

"Just fuckin' wonderful."

"You should cut down on the drinking," I say.

"I should do a lot of things," he says, "but you know what? She should lay off. She could do a lot worse than me."

I almost say it but I don't. Instead I tell him I'm going home and he gives me a lift. I can tell he's feeling a little bit better because on the way to my place we stop down at the wharf and he makes plans with someone about going lobster fishing on the weekend. Just before he lets me out in my yard, he tells me he's really going to try this time.

It's raining. Chuck is acting as foreman today so he drove us all out. We're deeper into the woods than yesterday and the smell of fir is thick. We huddle in the back of the truck and wait to see if the weather will clear. Alana is very quiet. Usually she joins us in a game of auction 45s but today she sits and stares out the back. Finally the rain lets up and Chuck stands in the doorway.

"Anyone crazy enough to work today?" he says, and offers his hand to Alana. She lets him help her down.

We pick up our gear and head out over the soggy site to set up the guidelines. Chuck says he wants Alana to show him how to do it. They walk on ahead and he helps her let out the twine.

That's the way the day goes. I work with Mike, have lunch with Beth, and watch Alana and Chuck. He's sticking to her like tar to railroad ties. He's helping her with her tree trays, or she's spraying him with bug spray or else showing him how to unjam the gun. Once I look up and see him massaging her shoulders. She tips her head back and closes her eyes.

I'm getting pretty disgusted. I can understand that he's hot for her, Alana does that to a lot of guys. What bothers me the most is that everyone else has noticed. Almost every planter has stuck a thumb in their direction and raised an eyebrow.

Finally our lines meet and Alana and I work side by side. I figure Chuck must have realized that it didn't look all that good to be sticking so close to Alana, because now he's working with Mike.

"Don't you think you're being a little obvious?" I say.

She says, "It doesn't matter now. I told Danny I'm leaving him."

I stop and stare at her. "Yeah?"

"I'm doing it right this time, though. This time I'm leaving town."

"Where to?"

"Toronto."

"Isn't that where Chuck's from?"

She nods, looking pleased with herself.

"Alana," I say, "let's stop for a break."

We sit on a log. She hums a tune and looks around at everything except me.

"Let me get this straight," I say. "You met this guy yesterday and today he's your knight in shining armour?"

"Of course not. You think I'm stupid?"

"Well?"

"I told him I wanted to move to Toronto and he said he could get me a job. Don't you see, he's my connection, that's all." She stands up and kicks at the dirt. "I'm doing it, Nancy, I'm getting the frig out of here."

"What about the kids?"

"They're out of school next week, so that's when we go."

"Shit, you mean it, don't you? What did Danny say?"

"What could he say?" she says. "He knew it was coming. In fact I think maybe he wanted it to happen. Hey, he probably has some hot one waiting in the wings anyway."

I have to laugh. "You're the only woman for Danny, Alana. You don't need to worry about that."

"Who's worried?" she says. "I couldn't care less at this point."

So now I'm sitting in the back of the truck waiting for Alana. I see her coming down from the hill. She has untied her braid and her hair flows around her arms. When she's near I swing open the door for her to climb in, but she waves her hand and goes around to the cab. Chuck's in there, waiting behind the wheel. I watch them through the little window. They're both laughing and Alana is flashing her very special smile. Mike is watching too. He says, "Lucky Chuckie." I close my eyes for the drive back to town.

Alana and I are at the Purple Hall. We drink beer and watch everybody. A band from the next town is playing some really good dance stuff. Billy Porter comes by our table and asks me to dance. I follow him up to the dance floor and out of the corner of my eye I see Chuck come in the door. I watch him go straight to Alana and sit in my chair. When the band plays a waltz, I thank Billy and leave the floor in time to see Chuck take Alana's hand as she gets up from the table. They go right by me and start dancing real close. And that's when Danny and Mike walk in.

Well, it's easy to see Danny's been drinking when he comes and sits with me, because he wraps his arm around my neck and gives me such a big kiss on the mouth that it hurts my teeth. He waves over to Mike but Mike doesn't seem to want to join us. Danny says, "Want to dance?" I shake my head. I see Alana leave the dance floor. She storms over to us. I look around for Chuck but I don't see him anywhere.

"Where the hell are the kids?" Alana shouts at Danny.

Danny doesn't even look at her. He just says to me in this real sad voice, "I hear Alana's been sluttin' around in the woods out there. Now, would you say that was true, Nance?"

I just look at Alana and she says, "Come on, Danny, let's go out and talk."

He stands up and looks at her like she's out of focus, then he pushes her hard, landing her in my lap.

"I just want to make one thing clear around here," he shouts at everybody who has stopped to watch. "She's not leaving me, I'm leaving her!"

He turns around real quick and runs sort of crooked out the door. Everybody starts laughing and Alana runs to the bathroom. I go outside. Danny is in his car and the motor is running.

"Danny!" I shout.

He throws the car into gear and the tires spin on gravel as he turns his head to back up. But the car doesn't go in reverse. Instead it smashes head-on into the building. The windshield breaks and Danny slumps over the steering wheel. The horn blares.

"Holy shit!" I hear someone shout.

"Someone get Alana!" I scream, and run to the car. In seconds everybody in the place is outside. I have the car door open but I don't know what to do. Blood is pumping from Danny's nose and mouth.

Alana and I are at the hospital. She has just left the room saying she had to go call about the kids. Danny is conscious now and wouldn't let go of Alana's hand until she promised to come back in the morning. All he has is a broken nose, that and two lost teeth. I put a glass of water to his lips and he sips at it. Then he closes his eyes.

I go out in the hall, where Alana sits on a bench. She seems kind of shaky so I hand her a piece of gum. We just sit there, snapping it away. A nurse we know comes by and shakes her head.

"He's a lucky guy," she says.

Alana says, "He's lucky I don't finish the job."

The nurse laughs and goes into Danny's room.

I mutter, "He's lucky to have you."

She snorts, "He's just lucky I'm not ready to lose him, yet."

"No more Chuckie?"

KNIGHTS

"My knight?" She stands up and puts her hands on the small of her back like it might be sore. "What a joke."

UP UNDER THE SUBWAY

Ricky has gone and let Tripper talk him into going up to Henry's house. Before we came out to the Purple Hall tonight, I made him promise we'd go home before last call. Now it's last call and Ricky has just asked Dennis for a double rye.

Up on the dance floor, three women still sway to some moaning blues song. They wear shiny dresses with slits up the sides and look like they're practising for a show. Tripper stands up and hoots, "Look at those girls go, think they're in New Orleans."

Ricky's just laughing. His eyes are all blurry, the way they always get when he's drinking. He yanks at Tripper's jacket sleeve until he falls back into his seat.

"Then let's go," Tripper says. "Sweet Rena Dickson said she'd be up at Henry's."

"Let's go home, Ricky," I say, but it's like talking to a barn door.

Tripper lifts a hand to his ear and says, "You hear a little squeak, Ricky? Sounds like a mouse, don't you think?"

Ricky laughs. "She's just watching out for me, that's all."

Everybody likes Ricky, but I love him. We live together in a big room above the Jupiter Restaurant, where I work part time. When we moved in last fall we painted the old wood floors a shiny blue, and I cut out some curtains from flowered sheets. Still, our place smells greasy from the restaurant. Tomorrow morning I have an interview at the best hotel in town, because they need a night clerk. The hours are lousy but the pay is good, I hear, and a lot of people will be trying for it. It would help if I was to get a good night's sleep.

The girls have stopped dancing and the house lights come on. Only a few people are left sitting at the sticky tables. Dennis tells us to get going, and goes over to poke at someone who's asleep in the corner.

Ricky says to me, "You go home if you want. I'm going up to Henry's."

But I'm not about to let him go alone up there with Tripper. Who knows, he could end up with Rena Dickson too. Rena with the buck teeth. The boys say God had them in mind when he made that mouth. I've heard that she'll get on the floor in the back seat of a car and do three guys, one right after the other. I'm not sure if that's true or just another legend, but I'm not about to let Ricky find out. When he's drinking he gets to thinking he's on some high adventure. Like the time he thought he could just borrow a fire truck for a couple of hours. That bought him a night in jail and a big fat fine.

My father is a town cop and thinks that Ricky is a loser. He says things to me like "What are you trying to be, some kind of Florence Nightingale? He's a drunk and a bum. Nothing you do for him is going to change that."

He doesn't care that Ricky is really an artist. At Chase's poolroom, where he works, he sits behind the counter and draws pictures. He drew one of Tripper leaning over the table, with his belly squished over the felt and his face all screwed up over a tricky shot. I can almost hear Tripper curse when he misses. At home, Ricky has a canvas propped up on a kitchen chair. He's doing a painting of me sitting naked at the table. It's nothing bad, either, I just sit with my smoke and tea and stare at the window. Sometimes I sneak a peek at him, because he has a face on that I never see any other time. It's drizzling outside the Purple Hall. Ralph Peterson drives by and Tripper whistles for him to stop.

"Let's go, good buddy," he calls to Ricky, as he runs over to Ralph's taxi.

"You coming or what?" Ricky says to me, right quiet like.

In Ralph's car, Tripper pulls out a rum bottle that he's had stashed inside his jacket and starts chugging away. Ralph passes back a cigarette smeared with hash oil and I take it. If I'm going to some party up under the subway, I'm not going straight.

The subway. All that really means is where Clarke Street goes down under a railway bridge. Once I went with my father up to Montreal for a week and there was a subway to see, and it wasn't just some dip in the road.

"Hey, Nancy," Tripper leans over Ricky and says to me, like he's really concerned. "You afraid old Ricky's going to end up with Rena, maybe? That why you won't let him off the leash tonight? Ha ha!"

He laughs so hard at his own joke that he starts coughing all over the place. Ricky slaps him on the back but Tripper keeps hacking and hacking.

"Do you think he'll choke to death?" I say.

Ricky nudges me with the bottle of rum. I shake my head, and when he tries to touch my hair I wave his hand away like he's a pesky fly. He has told me over and over that all Tripper is to him is a drinking buddy, but I say, "All?"

We turn up Henry's street. The houses around here are small and painted in soft colours. Kids' toys clutter up the front yards and the backyards are full of car wrecks. Farther up the hill is where the blacks in town live. I think some of those houses don't have glass in the windows, just nailed-on plastic.

At Henry's house there's mud all around the front step. We go in and I'm about to take off my boots but Joyce says, "I wouldn't do that if I was you."

I go into the kitchen and see what she means. They must have been fighting because someone has smashed a big jar of peanut butter all over the counter. Brown gobs stick to Joyce's window curtains. Broken plates lie like half-moons in the sink.

There's a poker game going on at the table. Ricky has already thrown in his ante. No one seems to notice that glass crunches under their boots. Joyce says from behind me, "He thinks I'm going to clean it up but I'm not."

"Then get the hell out of here, woman," yells Henry, who is sitting with a full house, I see.

Joyce says, "Come look what he did to the bedroom."

We go in. All the furniture is tipped over. You can't even see the floor for the stuff all over it. There's a woman lying on the bed. Her mouth is open and she's snoring.

"Pills," Joyce says. "She was sick. I came home from work and here she was. Know her? She didn't even wake up when all this was going on."

We close the door and go out to the living-room, where there are a bunch of people. Sid Ibsen and his brother and some stranger sit over by the stereo. No one's saying much. Tripper is sprawled on the couch and looks like he's asleep because his big red beard lies on his chest. Then I see he probably isn't because he's holding a lit cigarette. On the walls are paint-by-number pictures of dogs and ballerinas. Joyce sees me looking at them.

"I did those."

"Nice," I say, because I like Joyce okay.

"Want a beer?" She passes me one out of a case by the door. I stand there because I don't want to sit near Tripper. The stranger gets up and offers me his chair.

"I'm Curtis," he says. "Sid's cousin."

"Nancy."

"That's a pretty name," he says, giving me this big smile with these rotten teeth.

Then there's this big snort coming from the couch and all of a sudden Tripper drops his cigarette on the floor and bangs his boot down on it.

Joyce shouts, "For Christ's sake, Tripper, what do you think this is, a barn?"

"I dunno, Joyce," Tripper says with his eyes on the Ibsen boys and this Curtis. "Since when did Henry start letting niggers in this place?"

And it's like the room holds its breath and there's this ugly silence. The only sounds come from the kitchen. I can hear Ricky saying, "Hit me, hit me again! Aw shit!" — he never did know when to quit at blackjack.

Joyce stands there holding an ashtray and looking up at the ceiling. I just want to get out of there, because I know Tripper, and this guy Curtis is looking like he's about to kill him. Tripper starts laughing.

"Ha ha, Jesus Christ, Sid. If I'd known the whole Ibsen clan was coming here tonight, I woulda stayed downtown."

Sid just says, "Hey, if I'd known Tripper O'Leery was coming here, I would have gone home."

And it's like the room starts breathing again. Joyce puts the ashtray near Tripper's feet and pops the butt into it.

Nowadays, most white people here wouldn't call a person a nigger to their face. Once a black guy slapped a white girl for doing exactly that. A bunch of whites tore up the hill after him and the blacks didn't take too kindly to them tearing their houses apart looking for the guy. My father said the town cops couldn't do a thing about it. When it turned into a riot and headed down towards the subway, the RCMP were called in and finally broke it up. A lot of homes got wrecked that night, all of them up on the hill.

Tripper says he remembers this because he and his mother were staying up there with a black family then. He says they were turfed out after that night. He says he has just as much right to use that word as anybody.

"Well, I guess if you got to let them in your house they might as well be the Ibsens, right, Sid?" Tripper is saying.

I never could stand to hear Tripper egging on the Ibsen boys, so I go in and join the poker game. I guess Curtis has had enough too because he follows me out to the kitchen.

Well, there's nothing like poker to sober Ricky up. He gets this tense smile on his face and his foot starts jiggling up and down. I love playing poker with him because we usually clean up, but not tonight. Curtis has wrapped up the last four hands of seven-card stud. I can tell Ricky's trying to distract him because he keeps talking.

"Ya, tough town, Halifax is. Once had a job down there on the waterfront. Maybe you know some of the guys I worked with."

Curtis just nods and bumps up the stakes for the third time. I'm done for — a pair of jacks and I can see that all Ricky's doing is distracting himself. I start nudging his knee, so he tells me to go round up Tripper.

In the living-room I see Henry lying on the couch with his head resting in Joyce's lap. I guess they've made up because, by the way she's looking down at him sleeping there, you'd think he was her darling baby. When I ask where Tripper is, she points to the bedroom. I go in there just in time to see this girl pushing Tripper away from her. Now that she's awake, I recognize her. She comes to the Jupiter sometimes and orders soup and coffee.

When she staggers out of the room, Tripper says to me, "What are you looking at me like that for? She might never have woken up if I hadn't come along. I probably saved her life."

"Yeah, and now she's probably gone to puke."

Tripper yawns and smirks. "You know, you could use some waking up too."

By the time we're ready to go, everyone else has left. Joyce is in the kitchen picking up glass.

It's gotten all foggy out. We walk under streetlamps circled by mist. It's just under the subway that Curtis and the Ibsens are waiting for us.

"What's going on, boys?" Ricky says, but no one says anything and everyone looks scared. Then they surround Tripper.

Tripper laughs until this Curtis taps the top of a beer bottle off against a cement pillar. Above our heads a freight train rattles into town. Ricky slips into his referee act, which means he acts way drunker than he really is and tries to get in everybody's way. Sometimes it even works but not tonight. Sid grabs his arm. Curtis lands Tripper a karate kick or something which sends him to the sidewalk. Then he kneels over him and rests a point of the jagged bottle in Tripper's navel. Tripper's hairy belly is heaving up and down but he must be stunned because he doesn't move. He just stares up at Curtis, who's tracing a circle on his skin.

Sid's brother says, "Hey, somebody's coming."

Sure enough somebody is coming, but it's hard to see who it is in the fog. Sid squints his eyes up and says, "It's just Rena Dickson. Let's go now, Curtis, you got him good."

But Curtis doesn't stop his tracing, and he mutters something about pork belly just as Rena reaches us. She stares down at them. The only noise now is the jangling of her bracelets as she raises her hand to play with a piece of stringy blonde hair. She asks Sid what's going on.

"Tripper's been shooting his mouth off again at the wrong person. Curtis here is making dogfood."

"Oh," she says with a snort. "Curtis hates his dog?"

She pulls out a smoke and asks Sid for a light. He's been holding onto Ricky's arm and now looks glad to have an excuse to drop it.

Rena turns to me. "You going to that interview tomorrow?"

"How did you know?" I say. I hardly know Rena except that we were partners back in home ec. I remember her being more interested in sneaking off with the vanilla extract than in making muffins.

"I saw your name on the list when I went in there."

Sid says, "You talking about the night-clerk job? My sister's trying for it too. I told her not to be so stunned. That hotel never had a black girl working for them."

"Oh, I don't know, Sid," Rena says, "Marsha's real pretty. I bet she's the prettiest girl in town. Some smart, too."

"Yeah?" Sid says. "Yeah, she is too at that."

Then the weirdest thing, it's like the fog has lifted and there's this big change. We're standing around like it's Main Street at noon. Curtis must feel pretty silly to be admiring Tripper's belly the way he is, because he stands up, but not before giving old Trip a knee in the gut. It must have hurt, but Tripper doesn't show it when he hauls himself up. Rena just walks away.

"Where you going, Rena?" Sid says.

"Nowheres, maybe Super Subs, you want to come?" She nods her head at Curtis and Sid's brother. "They can come too."

We watch them walk into the fog and I hear Curtis tell Rena that she has a pretty name. I hear her laughing up the hill.

Tripper and Ricky and I stand there, just breathing, before we leave the subway and head on downtown. Tripper starts ranting about Rena and how she's blown it now with him since she'll probably take on all three of those Ibsens before the night is over.

I can't help it, I spin on him and stick my finger at his chest. "You're an asshole, Tripper! Rena just saved your hide."

Tripper laughs. "Did you believe all that back there? Sid wouldn't have let him do it. We used to be best friends. I can't help it if his cousin can't take a joke."

We're at Tripper's street and he turns down it, still talking like we're right beside him. "Yes sir, Sid's like a brother. I'm going to have a talk with that boy."

When I look back at him, he has stopped under a streetlamp and seems to be checking his belly.

All the way home, we don't talk. I figure Ricky has finally seen Tripper for what he is, so I go and say, "And that's your best friend?"

"You're my best friend."

"Come on, Ricky, you know what I mean."

He puts his arm around my shoulder. "I know you hate him and I know why. He doesn't give a good goddamn about anything or anybody. He doesn't even care if he dies — you saw him back there."

"No way, Ricky," I cry, "he was just scared shitless."

"Think what you want," he says, "but I see him as sort of free."

Well, that's Ricky for you. He also said once that, no

matter what anyone said about Rena Dickson, he just saw her as being one of the loneliest souls in town. Okay, maybe I can see that, but it doesn't mean I have to start hanging around with her. Oh hell.

When we get home Ricky wants to work on our painting, but I say no. Then I go and pull our bed out of the couch. Before Ricky goes to sleep, he takes my hand and kisses my fingers. I lie there, wide awake now. The Jupiter sign flashes bright as anything through the window, and through these tears which have come from somewhere. God, I need that job bad.

RIGHT INTO THE SCREAMERS

Carla and I sit in my car outside the bootlegger's and talk about Shell. She's in there getting some beer for all the WD girls back at her new apartment. It's Friday night and the liquor store is closed. Since Shell knows Kenny the bootlegger, she's the one who gets to go in. I'm driving because I'm the most sober and Carla wanted to come along for the ride.

"Think she'll go back to Darcy?" Carla asks from the rear seat.

"I don't know, hard to tell," I say and take a swipe at the windshield since it's all fogged up.

"You know she's worried he'll do something stupid, don't you?"

I have to laugh. "You mean something really, really stupid? Or regular everyday stupid?"

Carla sticks her elbows up on the back of the front seat and leans forward to look for Shell through the rain. "Well, she can't very well go back after tonight, now, can she?"

I turn the car heater up and the music down. Ever since Shell left Darcy she's been carrying about five tapes around in her bag and playing them real loud whenever she gets near a tape deck. She says there's nothing like the Stones to give you courage.

Tonight is Shell's surprise house-warming party. A bunch of us piled in there while she was at work and turned that little place into a home. Everybody brought something. Katrina Webber brought almost a whole dish set. I found two really nice scatter rugs on sale down at Morgan's. Lisa's grandmother died a while back, so Lisa had a rocking-chair and bureau trucked over this afternoon. Shell was so stunned when she walked in that she could only stand there with her mouth open until someone handed her a beer. Now she's got plants and pictures, candles and a lamp, even an old exercise bike.

"So's she can snag a man," Katrina said in a silly voice.

Shell laughed and said, "That's the last thing I need, girls, *the* last thing."

So now we're into partying. The girls were hooting it up when we left. Crissey Raines had brought along some real sleazy outfits from the second-hand store she owns, and some of the girls were putting on a fashion show for the others. We were laughing so hard we felt sick, especially when Katrina came out wearing a too-tight leotard and a jock-strap.

"We're all the wives of some drunk or other," Shell said, back when we began this whole WD stuff.

"Speak for yourself," said Katrina. "I think WD should stand for Women Drunks not Wives of."

"Who cares what we are?" Carla said, throwing her arms in the air. "Any way you look at it, we should do this more often."

Now Shell comes out of Jack's back porch and hops around the muddy driveway to the car.

"Shit," she says, as she gets in. "I just got my foot soaked all the way through my sock."

Carla starts in on her laugh at the way Shell has said this, and can hardly pull the beer into the back seat. She has this laugh and she uses it a lot. She makes everybody feel like they're real funny.

"What took you so long?" I say.

"What else?" Shell says. "Darcy."

"Darcy! He was there?"

"On the phone," says Shell. "He just happened to call Kenny for rum. And Kenny, being the dog he is, had to tell him I was there and hand me the phone."

"And of course you had to talk to him," says Carla. Shell plugs in the Stones again and blasts it up loud, shakin' and rockin' her head like she never even heard Carla.

Carla and I look at each other.

"And?" Carla asks.

"And he's right out of it, and laying this trip on me about the twins and how could I just walk out on them. God, I feel bad about them."

"You didn't leave them, Shell," I shout, and turn down the Stones. "You left Darcy, they know that. They're not blind, you know."

"But I'm worried about them, you've heard about the parties."

Carla pats Shell's shoulder. "You can't cover everything at this stage of the game, sweetie, only the basics."

It's about time Shell left Darcy. She's been trying for years. Once she moved back to her mother's place but it wasn't far enough. All it took was for him to straighten up his act for a while and pretend like he was courting her all over again. Darcy can be mighty charming when he has a mind to be. He can be just as nasty. I've heard him screaming at her when I was halfway up the street. She says he never hurt her, but I was there one night when he kept jabbing away at the middle of her chest with his finger until she fell back over a footstool. It's not all his fault, though, anyone can see that. Shell's been playing this good little wife and mother role so well that I think she was hoping this must be normal family life. The problem was, he never talked to her except when he was drunk, and then it was to tell her how stupid she was. And then she got a receptionist's job up at out-patients last summer and found she liked it. She was so good with patients that they actually felt better just from talking to her about things like the weather. Getting that job was good timing, too, because Darcy got laid off at the plant, like a lot of the boys did.

We're driving up Main Street and Carla gets this bright idea to stop at the Purple Hall. Shell and I tell her no way but she keeps it up. "Come on, I'll just run up there and see who's there."

As if there's apt to be any big change from any other Friday night. But I stop outside and up the stairs she charges, with her skinny little legs and wild red hair. She has a thing for Dennis the bartender.

While we wait, Shell tells me she and Darcy had a big talk last Saturday. He took her out for lunch over to the Truck Stop and then they went for a long walk along the dikes out on the marsh. I find this pretty amazing — not the thought of Darcy doing anything this romantic, he'll try anything, but mostly I'm surprised she didn't tell me this before. Come to think of it, she was kind of secretive when I asked her where she'd been on Saturday night. She told me she was helping her mother with her hair. Right. I don't know how I could have fallen for that. Anyway, it seems Darcy thinks Shell left him because of the WDs. He says that before the WDs they always managed to get through the bad times.

"So," Shell says, "I told him there never were any good times, only some not really terrible times."

"So what did he say?"

RIGHT INTO THE SCREAMERS

"He said, 'What ever happened to "for better or for worse"?' I'm telling you, he thinks I never would have left if it hadn't been for the WDs."

Shell's not the only one who's left her husband lately, and Darcy isn't the only one blaming the WDs. Danny called it the WD Disease after Alana threw him out of the house one day. Then Lisa left Mike. That really rocked the town, because Mike hardly ever drinks and no one could understand why she did it. The way she puts it, though, is that most women around town think that if their men weren't drinking, things would be okay. She says they're missing the big picture. She ended up going back to him, though, because he made some big changes and he's stuck by them so far. And he's even stopped giving her a hard time about hanging around with the WDs.

We're still waiting for Carla but neither of us wants to go up to get her. Darcy may be there, and my Ricky is bound to be there too. That Carla, sometimes she really pisses me off, always forgetting everybody else if Dennis so much as smiles at her. Finally I get pissed off enough and go on up. There she is at the bar, laughing at some dumb trick Dennis is doing with a matchbook.

Oh great, I see Ricky over on the dance floor. His eyes are closed like they always are when he does his drinking dance. He's dancing with some young girl I don't know. I can tell she thinks he's quite funny, even when she has to save him from bumping into things. I used to do that.

I go to the bar and yank Carla's arm. As we go out the door I turn around to see Ricky tumble into a speaker. At least it makes him open his eyes. He sees me and shouts, "Hey!" but we run down the stairs and out into the rain.

We stop at Damrey's store to pick up some chips and stuff and then Shell wants to drive by the house before we go back. We turn down Curry Street and crawl by the little house Shell has just walked out of. It feels strange to think she doesn't live there any more. It must feel real weird to her. Upstairs there's a light on in the twins' room. We can see Jarry up there, playing his electric guitar. A girl with long black hair passes in front of him and we see him toss his hair back as if he's laughing at something. They're good looking boys, those twins. They remind me of Darcy when he was younger and gathered girls like kindling. They're right into partying like Darcy is too. Only I guess since Shell left he's not so much fun now. In fact I heard he got right pissed off one night and threw the whole bunch of them into the street. Even his own boys.

Back at Shell's apartment the girls are right into the screamers. They're all dancing with their arms raised, and singing so loud we could hear them from out in the yard. Katrina's trying to get everybody to follow her in some kind of dance step but she's right the frig out of it, so you can just imagine. Carla jumps right in there, and that really gets them going because she has this energy and that laugh.

She's the one who started this whole WD thing. One hot Friday night last summer, she talked everybody into going out to Katrina's cottage at the shore. And we went without telling the boys what we were doing. By the time we got there, a storm was building up out on Northumberland Strait and we had the greatest time just sitting on the porch and watching it roll in. We sipped at rum and Coke and talked about old times and about stuff going on in town, and we didn't even talk about our men or kids for a change, until Alana all of a sudden said, "You know, I realized something the other day."

"What?" we all said at the same time, which made us hoot because Alana is known for coming out with just about anything.

She closed her eyes and said, "I realized that this is about as good as it gets."

But the way she said it was so serious that we all shut up.

"Up till now," she said, "I always thought something else would happen, something to change my life — you know, like when I had the babies, or like when we bought the store. But nothing's changed in a long long time. Maybe that was it, maybe nothing good will happen again." She set her drink down and got up and stood at the window with her hands stuck in the back pockets of her jeans. "And then there's Danny. He just sees me as someone who's going to make him a little more comfortable in his old age."

We all looked at each other. I mean, what could we say? Then Katrina got up and stood beside her. Shell went in to put on the Doors, the one with "Riders on the Storm". We turned off all the lights and watched lightning crackle through the sky and light up the whole strait. We watched Alana cheer up at the excitement of it all. Then we went down to the beach with a big fat joint and took all our clothes off. We jumped in the waves and screamed.

Well, on Monday when I went in for a check-up at Dr. Black's, her receptionist told me the boys had got pretty freaked out on Friday when they couldn't find their women anywhere in town. I guess they were going around asking everybody if they'd seen us. For once we weren't the ones chasing them down.

The dancing has cooled off a bit and we're just flopping around on the couch and the floor when there's a knock at the door. Shell goes to answer it and in rolls Ricky with some guy. I can't believe Ricky has the nerve to do this, even in the state he's in. He makes this big announcement, "This is Craig." He points and stumbles towards me with his eyes half closed. "And Craig, this here's the most beautiful woman in the world, Nancy McKinnon!"

"Ricky?" I say. "What the hell do you think you're doing here?"

Ricky says, "I was just telling Craig here all about you and I wanted him to see for himself. So Craig, didn't I tell you?"

This Craig, who looks like he's sobering up in a hurry, seems kind of nervous. I'm wondering if he's heard of the WDs. There's one of those dumb rumours going around town that we once held some guy down and wrote our names all over his dick. "Now, that's a good one," we like to say, "only it was more like our initials."

I stand up. "Okay, Ricky, so I'm the most beautiful woman in the world. Now you guys can just take off."

The girls are all laughing and Carla says, "Aw, can't we keep Craig, Nancy? He's real cute."

Craig backs out of the room and we hear the door close. Ricky tries to put his arms around me and I'm getting madder and madder. And I hate him. He's been on a three-day drunk and I can tell he's near the end of it by the heaviness of his arms on my shoulders. Tomorrow he'll be on a major suck which should last for, oh, a week or so. He'll be in awful bad shape for a day, lying in bed with a pillow over his head and wanting me to bring him tea and toast. Then he'll be as sweet as can be, sticking close to me like summer sweat. But as soon as he's strong enough to hear his good buddies calling out for him to join them, he'll start all over again.

"Come home with me?" Ricky whispers wetly into my ear.

The girls are watching to see what I'll do, and I have to do something or he'll spend the night on Shell's floor. I lurch to the door with him and he must think I'm coming, because he tries to bury his face in my hair. We step out onto the porch and I gently push him away. Then I step back inside and lock the door. I walk back into the room right calm, like I just put out the dog. The WDs are clapping so I take a bow, but what I really want to do is go look out the window. I try not to think of him falling down in the street in front of a car. Maybe I hate Ricky Chase, but I love him just as much.

Carla wants us all to drive over to the Truck Stop for some pie, but some of the girls have kids to get up with in the morning so we break it up. Shell and Alana and I go to get in my car but we find Ricky asleep in the back seat. He must have crawled in there when I put him out of the house. I'm all for throwing him right out, but Carla and Alana just lean him up against a door and we take off for the Truck Stop. It has stopped raining, and when we get out the stars are bright overhead and so are the lights of town back across the marsh.

The restaurant is pretty full. Everybody comes over from the Purple Hall after it closes, to sit under these lights that seem to turn skin green. That and the coffee'll sober up most anybody — at least you'd think so judging by the looks of them.

We wave at some people we know and then we sit and fiddle with the little jukebox at our table until we notice Carla all of a sudden looking like her hamster just died. I look carefully around the place and then I see the reason. It's Dennis, he's over there with his wife. I gathered from Carla's mood earlier that she had some pretty high hopes of seeing him here, alone. Poor Carla, in love with this guy for years. Every once in a while he'll throw her a bone and she'll chew on that memory for weeks. We tell her she should wisen up, he'll never leave Brenda, but Carla says that when he's with her, it's her he loves.

So when this guy Carla knows walks by on his way out,

she asks if she can catch a lift over town, and off she goes. She turns around and waves and laughs like she's not hurt one bit. We stay and eat our pie and talk about Carla. We think she'd be better off in a city somewheres.

We watch a sixteen-wheeler pull up and the driver comes in. He says to the waitress, "I guess that's some fire they're having over in town."

You'd think the fire was in the restaurant, it clears out so fast. Everybody stands in the parking lot looking over the marsh to town. We see orange flames shoot way above the ridge the town sits on. It looks so unreal that for a minute nobody moves. Everybody tries to figure out where it can be. All we can tell is that it's somewhere to the left of downtown. I look around at Shell but she's running to the car.

All the way back to town Shell keeps her hands on the dash and leans forward as if that will get her there faster. We tell her not to panic but we can see the fire straight ahead. It looks like it's in Darcy's neighbourhood. If it's not Darcy's house, then it's pretty damned close. In the rear-view mirror I see red lights flashing. They must have called in the fire department from Sackton. Two trucks come screaming past us and Shell is fighting back tears. We all feel the terror. Not Ricky, of course, he's fallen over into Alana's lap.

We get into town and tear down Curry Street. It's not Darcy's house, we see that now. The street ahead is crammed with cars and trucks so we pull into Darcy's driveway.

It's the big old Parker house, which has been empty for years. There are quite a few people standing around watching. Even Judge Guthreau is out there in his bathrobe. We get there just as the roof caves in. Shell starts crying and I think it must be out of relief.

Morning is coming around and we're all pretty tired now. Alana decides to walk home, and she slips into the crowd left standing around. Shell and I walk back to the car.

RIGHT INTO THE SCREAMERS

We get in and we're about to leave when Darcy's dog Cinder comes around the corner of the house and sniffs at a tree.

"Now, why do you suppose she's out?" says Shell.

Then we see that the side door of the house is wide open, which is strange considering the mosquitoes at this time of year.

Shell says, "I think I'd better go in there."

"No, don't, Shell," I say. "They just forgot to close the door, that's all."

"They're my kids," she says. "I don't care how old they are, I have to make sure they're okay."

"Well, do you want me to go in with you?" I say.

"I don't know. Maybe you're right. Maybe I shouldn't."

"I'll go in," I say, "you stay here."

I go in. Cinder follows me. The house smells right smoky. I turn on the hall light and go upstairs. The door to the twins' room is open a bit so I push at it. The light from the hall shines in on Toby where he sleeps soundly. Dirty clothes cover beer cases on the floor. This room smells like beer and pot and dirty socks. I look over at Jarry's bed. He's asleep too, and not alone. Curled in his arms is the girl with the long black hair. I see now that it's Alana's sister's girl. She must be all of fourteen. Oh boy, Shell will be thrilled to hear this. So will Alana. I open the window to the early morning air and the sound of nighthawks screaming in the trees.

I go down the hall to Darcy's room. His door is closed and Cinder whines and scratches at it. There's no sound so I open it carefully. Cinder slips through the door. I look in and at first I think the room is empty because there's no one in the bed, but then I hear Cinder's tail thumping on the floor and I look down. There's Darcy, lying on the floor, his body curling up around the dog. And that's when I see it, only I don't, because it's in his mouth. It's his thumb and I can tell by how his cheeks are moving that he really is sucking at it. I decide right there that my eyes are playing tricks. I close the door and run down the stairs quick.

Shell is chewing on her nails when I get back in the car. I tell her about Jarry and his friend but she doesn't freak out like I thought she would. She just says she'll have a talk with him. She doesn't even ask about Darcy. Just as well, I figure, but if it was me I'd at least want to know if he was alone. I think I would, anyway. I start the car and she plugs in a tape.

"You know," I say, "you should really take a tape deck from the house. That stuff is just as much yours."

"Yeah, I know," she says, turning the music down low. "But you know what? I feel better this way. Carla said I could keep hers for a while."

I drive her home and she gets out. "Thanks again for the scatter rugs," she says. "Call me tomorrow, or I'll call you."

"Sure, I'll call you tomorrow."

I drive home, listening to Ricky snoring in the back seat. For some dumb reason I start thinking about Darcy and his thumb. And every time I do I start laughing. I must be doing it out loud too because all of a sudden I hear Ricky say my name. Through the rear-view mirror I see he's trying to sit up, but no, there he goes, falling over on the seat again. Before I look back at the road I catch my own eyes in the mirror and I'm not laughing, after all.

GETTING OUT OF TOWN

It's been a pretty busy day out here at the Four Reasons Stop, even if it is November. Sometime during the night a fine dusting of snow settled over the roads and fields. I spoke to Ricky this morning and he said a good four inches came down there in town. A lot of people out here say the driving is bad, the snow being just enough to make a real slippery carpet to drive on. One guy who stopped for gas told me that he went off the road a few miles back but somebody in an old Land Rover yanked him right out of the ditch.

"Oh yeah," I said, "that was Bear James. He was in here a bit ago and told me he'd just hauled someone out."

"Well, whoever he is, he sure saved my day. Wouldn't take any money either."

"That sounds like Bear, that's something he would do."

In fact, Bear managed to haul me out of my ditch too. My ditch of a mood, that is. He told me a joke that went, What's red and sleeps four? The town truck, he said, and I had to laugh at that. Bitsey Quinn from down the road was in looking for vinegar and she said she didn't get the joke. Bear explained to her in that booming voice of his that the town truck was the public works truck, but I still don't think she got it because she just shook her head and left. Then we had a laugh over that too, until Bear said he had some cottage chimneys to sweep and he'd see me later. I watched him get in his Rover and drive on down the road. The sun had come out by this time and everything looked brown and wet. Bear James has been stopping in the store a lot more often these past two weeks, according to Alana, who has a way of narrowing her eyes when she says this. I have to laugh at her. She must think this will cheer me up.

Later Ricky calls back and asks me when he can come out to visit. I tell him he can get a lift on Friday with Alana when she comes home from work. I also tell him he can only come if he's sober.

It's been two weeks since I left Ricky and moved here to the Four Reasons Stop. At first I figured I'd drive in to work at the hotel every day. But then Alana said if I was really serious about leaving Ricky, maybe I should try staying out of town altogether. Why not trade jobs? The next day I told my boss I was quitting but that I had somebody really good to replace me. He said he didn't mind, since he thought I'd been acting a little too snarly lately. It's one thing if you're just a chambermaid, he told me, but hotel guests expect friendly desk clerks at least. He's right, the guests don't care that I'm exhausted from lying awake half the night waiting for Ricky to roll up the stairs. So it works out for everybody this way. Alana was going nuts being out here and said she was dying for the excitement of town.

"You think town is exciting?" I said one night about a week after I'd moved in, when we were sitting on the high stools behind the counter in the store.

She said, "Just you wait till winter sets in and you start going shack-wacky. Then you'll miss dancing at the Purple Hall."

That made Danny call over from the other end of the

store, where he was lying on the couch and watching TV, "What are you talking about, going dancing? I thought you said you were only going to be working in town."

"I'm just making a point, Danny," Alana said. "I'm warning Nancy here that even though she thinks she doesn't need to be around people, she might find she misses her old job."

Danny got up off the couch and came over to get a Coke out of the cooler. "Well, I don't see the difference between seeing people in town and seeing them out here. People are people, and you never minded the ones out here before."

He went back over to the couch and threw himself into it. All we could see were his feet hanging out one end, and his hand draped over the back. The TV blared out some cop show. Then ten seconds later he called out, "And I'd still like to know about this friggin' dance you're talking about."

"Dan, darlin'," Alana called over, "there really is no dance."

Then she winked at me and we snickered behind the counter, because we know how jealous Danny is of anything that takes Alana away from him.

That's how Alana came to be working at my job in town and how I came to be working at the Four Reasons Stop, which, by the way, was named by Danny soon after he and Alana bought it years ago. He thought the name was so clever he had Bear James make him up a sign the same day. I was out there at the time, helping Alana set up the apartment over the store where they'd be living, and we had just gone down to Beverley Beach with the kids for a swim after supper. It had been one of the hottest August days on record. When we pulled back into the yard the kids started cheering because the sign was up and surrounded by a string of blinking Christmas lights. Alana got out of the car and stood there tapping her toe and looking up at the thing. Then she shook her head and I could see she was trying not to laugh.

"So Danny," she said, folding her arms, "what are the four reasons, anyway?"

Danny, who we could see had been drinking a fair bit, swung his arm around and pointed to the pumps. "Well, there's the gas, and the store, and...."

"And?" Alana said.

"And ice," he said, swinging his arm around to the cooler by the door.

"That's three."

Well, Bear James, who had been standing there with a hammer in one hand and a beer in the other, just burst out laughing, the kind of laugh where the beer in your mouth somehow ends up in your nose, and he went wheeling around the side of the building.

"And what, Danny?" Alana said, not smiling any more.

"I'm just going to sell a few bottles to people I know, that's all."

"Aw, Jesus, Danny!"

Well, that set off a round of fighting that went on for a good week. Danny stuck to his guns and went about the business of bootlegging until all these strangers started coming and saying that So-and-so had sent them. Finally Danny got caught, and he just about lost everything over it — Christ, he almost went to jail. But he says the worst thing was having to listen to Alana go on about it every chance she got. She'd tease him something wicked, like the time he wanted to buy a motorcycle and was trying to figure out where he was going to get the money, and Alana suddenly snapped her fingers and said, "I've got it, we could start bootlegging! Eh, Danny? That way we could pay for this motorcycle we don't even need." It started to get on my nerves too, which is saying something, since there's not much Alana can do wrong

GETTING OUT OF TOWN

in my eyes. But Danny would get all pissed off, and I could tell she'd knocked the wind right out of his sails. Not for long, though — he's always coming up with something. Once he got this great idea to open up a little take-out restaurant in the summer. He set up picnic tables on the shady side of the store so hungry tourists could relax and enjoy the ocean view peeking up from behind rolls of hay and daisy-filled meadows. It was a good idea, only the flies on the Bradley farm across the road must have decided that what was dead on the plate was a better deal than what was live on the hoof, because they moved right in, buzzing all over the store and upstairs in the apartment. Even after Danny closed down the take-out and started working as the Bradleys' dairy man, they refused to leave, and to this day the store still has a fly problem.

No flies today, though, it being November. When Alana gets home, we go upstairs and make some rice with leftover ham.

Danny says, "What's the word in town?"

Alana says, "Not much, a lot more snow than out here."

"How was work?" I say. "See anybody interesting?"

"Yeah, I met this woman from out west. She'll be living in the old schoolhouse down there in Poplar for a while. She's different. I like her."

I don't say anything, but I guess maybe I sigh or something because Alana laughs and says, "You mean did I see somebody interesting like Ricky? Well yeah, come to think of it, he did drop in for a minute."

"Now, what would he be doing at the hotel?" Danny says, and pokes my arm. "You see what happens when the cat's away? I bet he was in there looking at that new blonde working in the lounge."

Alana swats him with her fork. "Actually, Dan dearest, he came in to give me something for Nancy."

GETTING OUT OF TOWN

I sniff at Danny as Alana gets up and goes over to where her coat is hanging. She pulls a rolled-up piece of paper out of the pocket and hands it to me. I carefully unroll it. It's a drawing of a bed. On it is the crocheted afghan I once made for Ricky. Under the afghan is one curled-up person. That person is Ricky, of course. He knows just how to get to me.

"Oh Danny," Alana says, leaning over to see it better, "look at what Ricky drew for Nancy. If I ever had the brains to leave you, would you draw a picture for me?"

Danny snorts and says, "Oh yeah, only I'd send one of me in bed with triplets."

"Ricky's always been so sweet to Nancy," she says, and turns to me. "Are you sure you want to risk losing him?"

I give her a look. She of all people should know what it's like to live with a drunk, no matter how sweet he can be at other times. That Ricky has just about convinced everybody that I'm the luckiest woman in the world. So many of my friends have said they wished they had someone who worshipped them as much as Ricky Chase does me. That's why I didn't make any big announcements about moving out of town. If anybody asks what I'm doing at the Four Reasons Stop, I say I'm just helping Alana and Danny out for a while.

The last time I saw Ricky, it was five in the morning. The evening before, he had left saying he was just going out for some smokes. I'd told him to pick up some ice-cream too because my father was coming for dinner. It was my father's birthday, and I had roasted a leg of lamb and Ricky had done the potatoes and turnip and peas. When my father came, the two of us sat around and talked for a while, with me looking out the window onto Main Street every few minutes until it was plain that Ricky wasn't coming. My father and I sat across from each other and ate supper and I brought out his cake and present, a ratchet set I got at Dave's Second-Hand Stuff. He didn't go on about Ricky the way he usually did, reminding

GETTING OUT OF TOWN

me how I was wasting my life with that bum, as he's always calling the man I love. But that night, when he was leaving, he put his hands on my shoulders and looked in my eyes, which likely looked like a couple of tidepools by then. Then he sighed and kissed me on the forehead.

When Ricky rolled in hours later, I was spitting mad. I don't usually shout at him because he just starts laughing at me, but that night I told him to get the hell out. I was so pissed off that when he put on this smirk I pushed him and he hit his head against the open closet door. He just looked at me and went over to the bed and sat on it. I stood there fuming and he closed his eyes for a long long time. Then he opened one eye and said, "Has anyone ever told you that you have a very nasty temper?" I started to shout, I opened my mouth to swear, but something else happened instead. My feet turned around and marched me to the closet where my suitcase was. Ricky lay down on the bed and watched as I stuffed the case with anything I could see that was mine. I didn't dare look straight at him, but every time I turned I could see him out of the corner of my eye, his dark hair lying against our white pillows. He'd gotten his hair cut the day before, just because my father was coming to dinner. By the time I was ready to go he was asleep, his freshly snipped hair resting jagged on his cheek. It reminded me of crow feathers and I wanted to reach out and smooth it against his skin. That didn't make it any easier to walk out, plus by then I was getting real tired and felt more like crawling into bed with him and letting him curl his body around me. In fact I was ready to drop my bag, but the weirdest thing happened — my fingers just wouldn't let go.

The sun wasn't quite up when I walked to my father's house and asked him if I could borrow his car to drive out to the Four Reasons Stop. He didn't ask me why; he saw the suitcase in my hand. I could have been heading for Toronto and he would have just nodded and handed me the keys. I got into the car and drove out to the store. I knew Danny would already be up and milking the cows across the road. Even Alana was up, opening the store. She acted surprised to see me, but she was running around in a flap because she had to go into town and that meant leaving the store. Seeing as I was there, she said, would I watch the store while she went into town to mail a parcel to her Kim down in Halifax?

"I never thought I'd be glad when the kids left home," she was saying as she went through the counter drawer looking for string. "But I was wrong. You know how much I worried about them when they were running the roads around here, well now I hardly think about them, and what a relief that is. I mean I think about them, of course, but since there's no way I can possibly know what kind of trouble they're into, I just don't worry...."

"Excuse me, Alana," I said, clearing my throat. "I happen to be pretty freaked out right now — if I could have a little of your attention?"

Alana put the parcel down on the counter and finally looked at me. "You mean this is serious? You really left? Just like that?"

"Why else do you think I'd be out here at seven in the morning?"

At least now I could talk about it. On the way out I could hardly drive for the blur in front of my eyes. Now that I was fifteen miles from town, I felt there was already a great distance between Ricky and me.

Of course, it's not over, eight years is a lot to snuff out, even if, as Alana likes to point out, we don't have kids. Every time we talk about what I'm going through with Ricky, she says, "You're some friggin' lucky you don't have kids, that's all I can say. You can't just leave when there's kids."

GETTING OUT OF TOWN

So Ricky comes out that Friday night. Earlier in the week, Alana had said she thought he looked a little tired and I had pointed out that Ricky isn't as young as he used to be. Now that he's here, though, I see what she means. His cheekbones look sharper, and dark circles hang under his eyes. This means he likely hasn't slept much since I left. I can tell he's been drinking hard, too, because his fork keeps clinking against the plate every time he touches it. Danny and Alana do all the talking. Ricky and I look at each other once in a while but it's almost like we're strangers, and it feels funny to think that only two weeks ago we were totally attached.

I plan on living in the trailer out back but it isn't fixed up yet, so for now I'm sleeping on the couch here in the store. Ricky brings his sleeping-bag in from Alana's car and rolls it out onto the braided rug. I feel sorry for him because he has a bad back and the floor is sure to be cold but he says it's just fine, we can pretend he's my dog, who would rather be on a hard floor beside my couch than anywhere else. We lie there like that, with the stove fire crackling and a red glow from the grate shimmering across the ceiling like the Northern Lights. Just as I'm drifting off, I hear Ricky whisper, "I miss you, Nance." And all I do is pretend I'm fast asleep.

The next day, when Ricky asks me when I think I'll be coming back, I ask him, "Why isn't anyone taking this move of mine seriously?"

I crook my finger at him to follow me and I lead him out back to where the red trailer sits surrounded by a bunch of young spruce. We go inside. Danny had put in an old oil stove when they used to live in it. The stove takes up a lot of room but he tells me it pumps out a lot of heat.

"Look, Ricky," I say, "this is my home now."

I show him the view from my two windows. One faces a corner of the store and looks down the highway. Through the other I can see across the fields and woods to past the strip of red cliff that holds back the ocean. I look at Ricky's hands resting on the windowsill. I love his hands, I used to just stare at them, at how the hairs rest so smoothly on the backs of them. I want to touch them, but instead I look out the window at my new view.

"You know, I still don't get it," Ricky says. "For eight years you stuck by me through things a lot worse than missing your father's birthday. And then wham, you just take off like that."

"You know something, Ricky?" I say. "I don't understand how we could be cooking a dinner for my father's birthday and *you* could just take off like that."

"So I guess I'd better quit drinking, and then you'll come back?"

"First let's see if you quit."

"Oh, I'll quit, you'll see."

"Okay, so we'll see."

"No, you will see," he says, frowning. "I know I can do it."

"Well do it for you," I say, "not for me."

In the store, Alana and Danny are watching the hockey game on TV. Alana gets up and pours us some tea from the pot on the stove.

During a commercial, Danny stretches his arms and yawns. "So what do you think, Rick — suppose she can stand living out here without you?"

Ricky smiles at me and says, "Well, Dan, I'm crossing my fingers. I have to tell you, though, I never thought I'd get rid of her."

"Ha ha ha," Alana says as we both get up and leave them to their little joke. We go to the other end of the store and sit on the stools behind the counter. Alana pulls out the gas receipts from the day and we add them up.

GETTING OUT OF TOWN

"You don't mind giving Ricky a lift into town tomorrow?" I say.

"Oh, he's going back to town?" she asks.

"Of course he is," I say. "What did you think?"

"Oh, I don't know," she says, and now that I see her face I can tell she's teasing me. "It's just that I thought the whole reason you moved out here and gave up your job was because you were leaving him."

"So?"

"Nothing," she says, "nothing at all. I guess you'll be sleeping with him tonight, then?"

"I don't know," I say. "I guess I might."

"Hmm."

"Well, what would you do if you were me?" I say. "You know there was a time when you were leaving Danny every second day, practically."

"Exactly," she says, "and that's because every time he got sweet on me I'd bounce right back into bed with him. And that, me dear, was the big problem."

I'm in my new bed in the trailer, and I am alone. Ricky and I spent the day getting it ready. We hung up old quilts on the walls to keep out the drafts, and Ricky even built a small porch outside the door so I won't have to step out onto the ground. I read my book and listen to the wind whispering through the spruces. It feels strange to think that Ricky is in the store on the couch, not fifty steps away. He wasn't too happy when I broke it to him that I was coming out here alone. He said he had been quite excited about the idea of sleeping in here with me, and what was the big deal anyway, this wasn't for keeps, was it? When I said that would depend on him, he looked up and smiled, but the smile only came out of one side of his mouth. That's how I know he's worried. In the morning he'll go into town with Alana and I'm not sure when I'll see him next. I wish he was in my bed. I wish he had his arm around me and his leg curled over mine, so I could look down from my book every once in a while to watch his eyelashes flicker from some dream.

    I read my book. It's about this California surf girl who becomes a Buddhist nun. The problem is that she goes and falls in love with a monk. I'm thinking that, even though her life is totally different from mine, right now my own life doesn't seem one bit more familiar.

In the morning I wake up early to the sound of Alana's car starting. Then I hear the car door slam, and I hear the car turn down the highway towards town. I'm feeling kind of proud of myself that I didn't let Ricky sleep in here after all. For one thing, I look around this little trailer and I realize that it's all mine. For another thing, I like it that I'm all alone. I get out of bed and dress real quick because it's some friggin' cold in here this morning. I light my oil stove and have my cereal at my table while I look out my window. I love my view of the water.

    Around noon I'm sitting in the store, munching on a sandwich and talking to Danny, who has come over from the farm for lunch. I happen to look out the window to the highway and I see this house moving slowly along the top of the horizon. I blink twice and say, "Danny, tell me what you see out there." As I look around the countertop for my glasses, Danny says, "Oh, yeah, the Hastings house. I forgot they were moving it today."

    He tells me how the Hastings move their house whenever they fall out with their neighbours. Which they always do, I guess, no matter where they move it to.

    "You'd think they'd learn something from that," I say.

    "Oh, I don't know," Danny says while we put on our coats, "they fight with each other all the time but you don't see them splitting the house down the middle. True love, I guess."

We go outside. It's a whole house, all right, and it really is moving, because it sits on top of a flatbed truck. A bunch of cars creep along behind it, since the house is too wide for them to pass. It's like watching a parade, the way they all crawl by the store. The driver of the truck rolls down the window and I see now that it's Bear James. He takes off his cap and waves it high like he's in a rodeo. His hair whips around his sunglasses and he whistles through his teeth. Danny shouts at him to come by tonight.

"Okay, good buddy," Bear shouts back. "I just have a small delivery to make." He jerks his thumb back at the house and grins.

"And good-day to you, Miss Nancy," he says, and tips his hat before he settles it back on his head.

I stand there and stare at the truck as it drives by. I can see Bear looking back at us through his rear-view mirror. Miss Nancy. I can't believe he called me Miss Nancy. His white teeth flash into the same grin he had back when I was fourteen.

Ricky phones and asks me when I might be coming into town. I tell him that I may come in on Saturday to go to the library. He says he'll work out something so he doesn't have to run the poolroom that day. I tell him not to change any plans for me, but if I have time I'll come by the apartment.

The next day I finish my book. The surfer who turned into a nun managed to fall out of love with the monk when she finally realized that, in order to find what she was really looking for, she would probably have to give up sex. So she did. She gave it up and the book ends with her sitting all content under a tree.

I leave the book on the counter while I go around back

to the trailer to check on the stove. When I come back I see a green Volvo wagon sitting at the pumps. Nobody's inside it, so I go in the store. There's a strange woman with long black hair nosing around the canned goods. She has to be wearing the brightest coat I have ever seen. Whoever made it must have used every colour in the world because, to me, it looks like a box of melted crayons.

These soft brown eyes look up at me and she says, "I don't suppose you have any fresh garlic?"

"We have powder."

"Oh, I read this," she says, picking my book up off the counter. "What did you think of it?"

I haven't really thought about what I think about it, since I usually read a book without thinking too much. She stands there like she's waiting for me to answer, though, so I say, "I don't know, I kind of liked it at first but I thought the last part was quite boring."

She laughs. "Really. I agree, take away the sex and what is there left to talk about?"

I ring in her garlic powder. "That's five seventy-five."

"Whew," she says, "not cheap."

Alana comes in just then, and I'm glad to see her. I'm not used to telling strangers what I think about things.

"Hi Nance — oh, hi Rachel," Alana says. "How's it going at the schoolhouse?"

It always surprises me how Alana knows everybody. Not only that but she can tell you who they're related to, how their babies were born, and whether anyone in their family has done time. This must be the woman Alana said she met at work.

"Good," she says. "I finally got someone to fix my roof, some guy named Brendon James? Do either of you know him?"

Alana and I try not to laugh.

GETTING OUT OF TOWN

"Brendon?" Alana asks. "He told you his name was Brendon?"

"That's not his name?" Rachel asks, looking confused.

"That's his real name," I say, "but everyone calls him Bear."

"Oh," says Rachel, "I get it, it's because that cabin of his is so deep in the woods."

Alana and I look at each other. Alana says, "You've been to Bear James's camp?"

"Yes," Rachel says slowly. "Um, is there something I should know about this guy?"

Alana says, "No, no, you won't find a nicer guy around. It's just that he doesn't usually have many visitors down there, that's all."

"Oh," she says, "I just visited it to see if it was worth painting."

"You're painting his camp?" I say.

"Actually, I find it quite interesting," she says, giving me this big smile. "Well, I guess I should get going. Nice meeting you, Nancy."

"Sure," I say.

"Come by sometime," she says. "It gets lonely out there, especially at night."

Alana says, "We'll stop by when we're out for a drive, right, Nance?"

We watch as she starts up the Volvo and turns onto the highway. Alana waves at her out the window.

"Do you suppose she's screwing Bear?" she says, twirling a strand of hair through her fingers.

I say, "Now why would he get somebody like her to paint his camp?"

"No, Nance, she's doing a painting *of* his camp," Alana laughs. "She's an artist. I wonder what it is she finds so interesting about an old camp in the woods."

"Probably all the windows," I say.

"The windows?" she says. "When did you ever see Bear James's windows?"

I yawn and pretend I'm looking for something under the cash register. There's a legend that no woman has ever set foot in that camp in the woods. Just last week Danny was going on about it, when he was talking to Bear and some of the boys here in the store about going out to the camp once hunting season starts. Danny loves to rub it in, too.

"Yessiree," he said. "You have to have all the right parts to go into those parts, right, Bud?"

Bear just laughed. "A man's got to have some peace from all you ladies once in a while."

"Oh, yeah," said Alana, rolling her eyes, "like the ladies are beating a path to your door."

Now that I've mentioned the windows, of course Alana won't let it drop. When I tell her I must have heard about them from one of the guys, she doesn't believe me for a second. Then I tell her that it was no big deal, I was at Bear James's camp a long time ago, just for a few minutes, back when I was hardly what you'd call a woman. Then I change the subject and say, "Who is this Rachel woman anyways?"

Next Friday night my friend Shell and her new boyfriend, Patrick, pull up around nine. Danny turns up his stereo and the beer comes out. At ten o'clock he flicks off the Four Reasons sign, but just as he pulls down the blinds someone bangs on the door. "Get rid of them!" Alana shouts, but it's Bear James. He pulls out some of his best homegrown and we all get silly and start dancing and singing until Alana gets wasted and goes to bed because tomorrow she has to open the store, since it's my day off. We end up the night by pulling out the cards and playing 45s until five-thirty, when Danny has to go across to milk the cows. By then Shell is sober enough to drive, so she and Patrick drive on back to town.

When Bear goes to leave he walks over to me and gives me this friendly hug that makes me remember how big he is. But when he runs his hand up my back and it makes me shiver, I try to pull away.

"Uh-oh," he says, rubbing my back with both hands. "I'd better warm you up, Miss Nancy, you're shaking."

I push him away for sure now, and he steps back, holding his hands up.

"Okay, okay," he says with this big grin, "I just thought that maybe, you know."

"That's twice you've called me Miss Nancy," I say, turning away. "You called me that the other day when you were hauling the house."

"What's wrong with 'miss'?" he says. "Is this one of those feminist things?"

I can feel my face getting kind of hot. If there's one thing I can't stand, it's me blushing. So I don't say anything. I just turn away.

"I was thinking maybe you needed company," he says, looking down at his cap. I stand there and watch his hands twirl it around. He reaches for the door. "Well, I'm around if you need me, that's all."

I can't sleep. It's cold in the trailer and dawn is peeking in through my curtains. Whenever I think of Bear running his hand down my back and me shivering like I did, I — well, I shiver some more. I feel like I'm fourteen again. Once I had such a crush on Bear James that I saved all my babysitting money and bought him at the YMCA slave auction. It was a fund-raising thing. Whoever you bought had to do what you wanted for a whole afternoon. We drove around in his Buick Skylark. I was the happiest girl in town, just to be sitting and riding with Bear James, who was almost twenty and could probably have had any woman in the world.

Alana bangs on my door to tell me that Ricky is on the phone. I look at my clock. It's only ten. I wrap my blanket around my shoulders and stick my bare feet into my boots. There has been a frost overnight and everything is shining bright, bright, bright as I tramp around to the store. The bell over the door seems to clang louder than usual. I take the phone from Alana, who's laughing at me. My mouth feels all shrunken and dry.

"Ricky?" I say, squinting because the sun through the window is really bugging me.

"Hi," he says, sounding just as bright as everything else seems to be around here.

"Are you okay?" I say.

"I'm finer than I've been in a long time, I can tell you that. I guess I'm not used to waking up on a Saturday morning without a hangover. What's wrong with your voice?"

"Oh, nothing," I say, clearing my throat. "I uh, just woke up. How come you're calling so early?"

"I figured you'd be up already."

"Yeah, well, Shell was out last night and we ended up staying up late."

He laughs. "That's a switch, eh? You drinking and here I went to bed before midnight. Anybody else out?"

"Oh yeah, her boyfriend from over on the island. Patrick? Is that his name? He seems okay, you know, I think they're good together."

"That's great. So what did you do all night, just talk and play cards?"

"Yeah. Look, Ricky, um, I'm really tired and...."

I look down at a note Alana has been scribbling and now sticks in front of my face. It reads, *I was already talking to him and I told him Bear was here.*

GETTING OUT OF TOWN

"Oh," I say, looking at Alana, "I almost forgot, Bear James was here too. They all left around five, so yeah, I'm tired."

"I just bet you are," he says, like he's chewing on a thought. "Well, maybe you can catch up on your sleep tonight."

"Tonight?" I say.

"Remember? You're coming into town. I was just wondering when."

I look at the clock again, and realize I have totally forgotten.

"I don't know yet, Ricky, why?"

"No reason, I just wanted to show you something."

"What is it?"

"Surprise."

"Okay," I say, "but remember I'm staying with my father."

We hang up. Awake now, I flip my hair out of my face and sip at the tea Alana has made for me.

"So why weren't you going to mention Bear?" she asks.

"I just wasn't," I say, while I fiddle with the chocolate bars on the shelf by the counter.

She says, "Is there something going on that I should know about?"

"No way," I say, like she's nuts to think there might be.

"Okay," she says slowly, "is there something going on that I shouldn't know about but you're going to tell me anyway?"

"No," I say, blowing at my hair to get it out of my face. "Nothing is going on."

It ended up taking me a lot longer to get into town than I expected, because Danny and Alana decided to have a big fat fight right around noon. It was something about a customer who owed a lot of money and, even though they had both agreed not to sell to him any more, Danny did anyway, when he was watching the store for me while I was upstairs making lunch. So Alana was hopping mad about that, and Danny, who usually tries to stay out of her way until she cools down, decided he had stuff to get off his chest too. So there I was, sitting down in the store listening to them upstairs, and I could hear Alana call him everything from a coward to an asshole, and then he started in about me. I heard him say something about them just finally getting the kids off and she had to go and turn the place into some kind of foster home. That really pissed me off since I'm not all *that* much younger than they are. But it's true that lately I've noticed Danny getting a little sulky every time Alana and I go off for a walk or drive together.

"The foster child can hear every word you're saying," I couldn't resist calling up the stairs, "and so will the customer who just pulled in."

"See?" Danny said as he clumped down the narrow stairs. "I can't even fight with my fucking wife in privacy!"

He stormed outside and got into the truck and took off up the highway towards town. So much for a lift to town.

I went up to see Alana. She was throwing some clothes into her little portable washing machine.

"I hate him," she said. "Really he is such a baby. If he doesn't get my full attention, he's ready to just walk on out." She slammed down the washer cover and dried her hands on her skirt. "You still planning on going into town?"

She told me that if I was to see Danny in town, I should tell him to pick up some toothpaste and on his way home to stop in at Jonson's Garage to make a payment on the snowblower.

I ended up hitch-hiking into town. Lucky for me, George Berkley picked me up. Lucky for him, too. He's the mailman and having someone sitting in the passenger seat makes life a whole lot easier for him. This way he just pulls up to the mailbox and I can roll down the window and pop the mail in, without him having to get out of the car. Of course the ride in takes longer than usual, but it's worth it not to be standing out in that wind off the water. Mostly we talked about my father. He told me a story about how my father saved his neck not long ago. It seems he ran a red light and my father could tell he was drunk as the ace of spades. Instead of running him in, though, my father just told him to leave the car where it was, and he gave George a drive home.

"Not without a lecture, I'll tell you that. He chewed me out like I was seventeen. And I'll never forget it, either. I could have lost my job right there. Darn near changed my mind about the law, I'll tell you that."

Then George asked if me and Ricky were going to the Purple Hall later. He said he heard there was a real good band playing tonight from Moncton. I guess the word hasn't yet gotten out to everybody that I'm not with Ricky any more. I noticed George looked at me kind of funny when I asked him to let me and my backpack off at my father's street, so I told him I had moved out to the store.

He said, "That right? Rick out there too?"

"No, he's not."

"Oh, I get it. Well that's too bad," he said. "You two seemed so good together."

"Yeah, well, we were, it just wasn't...."

"Never mind," George says, holding his hands up and turning his head away, "none of my damned business anyways. Say hi to your father for me, okay?"

I make some lunch for my father and we sit around for a while talking about what's going on in town. A lot of businesses are closing up and more people are out of work. This worries my father because this town is his whole life. It's like he's married to it. I wish he'd find a wife or someone just to do things with.

"Mind you," he says, straightening a picture on the wall, "I've seen it go through a lot of changes, and it always manages to come through somehow."

I notice how grey and thin his hair is now and how he always looks so tired.

My father just retired last April, and it's funny to think he's not a cop any more. He even made it to chief a few years back. There was a big party for him but Ricky and I were at a bluegrass festival down in the valley. Ricky was turning thirty and all I remember is it got so dark at night we were falling all over the field looking for our tent.

One of the first things my father did as police chief was to haul Ricky in because he'd climbed up on the cenotaph and sat on the soldier's shoulders, shouting at everybody who walked or drove by the park. I remember that night because I spent it pacing and smoking. Here he was in jail, for Christ's sake, and my father hadn't even bothered to phone me. When I asked him the next day why he couldn't have called to let me know Ricky was in jail, he just reminded me that Ricky could have called himself if he'd wanted to, since he was entitled to a phone call. Then he reminded me that it was my choice to live with a bum.

The next day, Ricky tried to make a joke about why he didn't call me from jail. He raised his hand and I saw that it was bandaged.

"You see?" he said. "What's that joke about not being able to call because of a broken finger?" He told me he'd broken it when he fell off the cenotaph.

The phone rings, and it's Shell saying that she spoke to Alana and she told her I was in town. She wants me to come to the Purple Hall with her tonight, since Patrick isn't coming over this weekend. I tell her I doubt I will, since the

Purple Hall is one place I can do without. Then I tell my father that I'm going over to visit Ricky and he says, "But you're staying here tonight, aren't you?"

I go downtown to the old apartment above the Jupiter Restaurant. It seems funny to knock on my own door but I tell myself it's no longer mine. Ricky opens the door and stands there looking more like he did when he was twenty-seven than he has for the last eight years. He has paint on his hands, too, which is something I haven't seen for a while.

"Close your eyes," he says, and when I do he lays his wrists on my shoulders so as not to get paint on me and he steers me into the room. "Now open them."

I look. There on his easel is a brand-new painting. It looks a bit like the big elm that stands alone down near the edge of the marsh, but all around it these colours wiggle and jump like they're the wind.

"This looks different than your usual stuff," I say.

"I'm trying something new."

"Oh," I say, looking around the apartment. Except for here where he's been painting, it looks quite clean and tidy, which means that he's been telling me the truth about not drinking lately.

I smile. "It looks like you're doing pretty good here without me."

"That's only because I want you to come back," he says, with that dark look that just about makes me think I want to do exactly that. He wipes his hands on a wet cloth. "You want some tea?"

We drink tea and I tell him about what's going on out at the store, but I don't tell him about Danny taking off for town this morning. I don't want Ricky to know that Danny is getting tired of having me living out there. Then Ricky pulls out my old chess set from under the couch. I forgot it when I moved out. My father gave me that set on my tenth birthday. The pieces are made of brass, and I see that Ricky must have shined them lately because the last time I saw them they were pretty tarnished. When we first started being together we'd play chess all night long. I got so excited playing those games that my heart would race and I'd almost lose my breath waiting for Ricky to make his move. It would be dawn by the time we finally reached for each other instead of the pieces.

We're in the middle of a good even game when there's a knock on the door. Ricky goes to answer it, and there's that woman Rachel who was out at the store that day. I see that she's wearing these torn brown overalls that match her eyes exactly.

"Hi there," she says in a cheery voice that I don't like the sound of. I see her slip something into Ricky's hand. "I brought you the Burnt Sienna."

"Thanks," Ricky is saying in his usual friendly voice, but I'm wondering why my heart is pounding. I put my tea down on the chest in front of the couch. What the hell is Burnt Sienna, anyway?

"Come on in," says Ricky. "I want you to meet Nancy."

"Oh hi," says this Rachel, and I notice that her teeth are perfect. "I met you out at the Four Reasons Stop, right?"

"That's right," I say. I look at Ricky, who's looking down at whatever it is in his hand.

"What's that?" I say.

"Paint," he says, smiling down at a small orange tube. "Rachel brought me paint."

I'm at the Purple Hall. I'm sitting with Shell and Katrina. Over by the dance floor I see Danny and Bear James leaning against the wall. When I came in I gave Danny Alana's message to pay the snowblower bill and he got all pissed off, saying Alana comes in to town every day so why couldn't she stop and make the payments for a change? And then he mumbled something about the fact that a man couldn't come to town without some woman bothering him, and he turned back to the bar. Bear asked me to dance and I said later, maybe. So by now I'm on my third rum and Coke. Katrina is right the fuck out of it, and getting to the point where either I have to drink more to catch up to her or else I have to leave the table because she's getting too crazy. Already she has knocked two glasses off the table, and Dennis, who isn't nearly as nice to us since he bought the Purple Hall is getting real ticked off at her. She'd better watch it. If he bars her, where'll she go?

Shell asks me how it's going out at the store, if I like being out there and all. I tell her that I love walking down to the beach, even if it is starting to get pretty cold down there, and that I like my cosy trailer where I can curl up under my red-and-blue quilt and read my books in the soft warm light from my lamp on the table. I tell her I like the privacy. What I don't tell her is that I'm bored out of my tree, and that all I do is mope around thinking about Ricky and me.

After Rachel left Ricky's place this afternoon, I asked him right off what was going on with her. He said that Rachel was teaching him a lot about painting. I said since when, and he said she'd been coming around for a week or so. I said I thought it was strange that he hadn't told me about her and he said he'd gotten the impression from me that he was supposed to be getting his life together without me. Then I yawned and said that I thought I should get going, that I was going to cook my father some dinner. As usual, the yawn gave me away. By now, he knows when I'm nervous. He kissed me and said there was nothing going on between him and Rachel. And then he put his arms around me and we stood like that until I could feel that things would get hot at any second, and I pulled away and went to my father's house to make meatloaf.

At first I'm jumping all over the dance floor with Bear James, and the next thing I know I'm pressed against him in a slow dance. For such a big boy, he's a good dancer, the way he moves to the music. I'm a little bit drunk, to the point where I'm stepping on his toes and laughing about it. He's laughing too. I'm even drunk enough that I almost don't give a shit when out of the corner of my eye I see Tripper O'Leery come in. I pull away from Bear, right in the middle of "House of the Rising Sun", and go back to my seat. Shell is leaning on her elbow talking to some stranger, likely one of the guys in town for a ball tournament, and Katrina is passed out, her chin tucked down into the collar of her blouse, her head bobbing up and down every so often. I'm wondering if Ricky is going to come in any second. I wouldn't be surprised. Ricky and Tripper usually run together, just like Danny and Bear do. I wave to Tripper, which shows what kind of state I'm in because normally I try to pretend he doesn't exist. He comes to our table and slobbers all over Shell and she frowns at me. Then this guy she's been talking to gets up and shoves Tripper, so of course we get an instant fight practically on top of us. This wakes Katrina up, and Shell and I pull her out of her chair and we go get our coats.

We've outgrown the fights. We used to just move out of the way and watch, but after a few years we realized they're all pretty much alike. When a fight breaks out, all the guys' buddies try to break it up. The crowd moves from one end of the bar to the other, following the fighters. Their girlfriends stand and scream at them to stop, tears ruining their makeup. Either the buddies manage to separate the fighters and calm them down, or they get all fired up themselves and start fighting with each other. That's when the police get called in and that's usually the end of that. It used to really bother me when my father showed up to break up the fights. It was just too weird to see him in action. It wasn't that he had to get rough — he could just push his way into the crowd and start telling everybody to break it up. And usually they would, too. I've heard that he could get pretty nasty if he had reason to, and I guess everybody else must have known that too. One thing I know for sure, the next day I would get a talking to and he would tell me the same thing over and over, that I was headed in the same direction as everybody who went to the Purple Hall — straight down the drain.

Shell and I stand on the steps outside. Katrina has gone around to the side of the building to pee. She's so drunk she likely won't notice how cold it is. Shell starts talking about everything she has to do for Christmas. The twins may be almost all grown up but she still gets right into it for them, dreaming up ways to surprise them. I can tell she's feeling guilty because she spends so much time with her new boyfriend. It doesn't do any good to remind her that the boys don't need her now like they may have when they were seven, but then she hits me with "You don't know, you have no idea, in some ways they need my attention more than they ever did."

Danny comes out the door and stands there rubbing his hands in the cold. Katrina comes around from the side of the building. Danny laughs at the sight of her, and she throws her arms around him.

"Oh boy, Katrina, I think I'd better get you home," he says, propping her up and weaving with her over to his truck.

"You're not driving home, are you, Danny?" I call out, because I know he's pretty drunk too.

"No way," shrieks Katrina. "I'm gonna take him home and fuck him silly, he's so cute."

"Promises promises," says Danny. "Do you think Eddie'll move over for us?"

"Eddie? Eddie won't even wake up!" We hear Katrina shriek before Danny slams his door and they drive off.

"Ooooh," says Shell, "think there's a chance?"

"Danny and Katrina? No way," I laugh. "But you know Katrina, she won't let him get away without a good-night kiss."

"Or two, or three," says Shell, standing there blowing her breath into the damp air. It's getting cold out here, but just as we turn to go back inside the door bangs open and Bear James comes tumbling out, and lands on the porch with this big *oooff!* coming out of him because Tripper O'Leery has landed on him. Bear gasps for air until Tripper rolls off him and manages to stand up. He grabs ahold of Bear's hand and pulls him up too.

"Ha ha, sorry about that, bud," Tripper says.

"Jesus Christ, I try to do the guy a favour and he trips halfway down the stairs," says Bear, bending over to pick up his cap.

"You're getting too old for this, you know," says Shell. "We get guys like you all the time up at out-patients, all banged up from being drunk and idiotic. It's pathetic."

She stomps down the steps and pulls her scarf around her neck. She shouts back at us, "I hate this town!"

I'm in Bear James's Rover. I have just asked him to drive down Main Street because I want to go by Ricky's place.

Back on the steps at the Purple Hall, Tripper couldn't wait to tell me that earlier in the evening he'd seen Ricky with that artist girl, having coffee in the Jupiter Restaurant.

Bear said, "You mean Rachel, who lives out by me?"

"Yeah, that one," Tripper said, spitting over the railing. "She's been visiting old Ricky quite a bit these days, I notice."

When I didn't say anything and just stared straight ahead

like I usually do when Tripper's around, he said in a louder voice, "Of course that doesn't mean anything to Nance here, seeing as she walked right out on Ricky. Yup, I wouldn't be surprised if old Ricky's doing the deed right now as we talk."

That's when Bear took hold of my arm and pulled me down the steps, whispering, "Never mind, you know how he makes life up as he goes along."

"Ha ha ha," I could hear Tripper laughing. "That Ricky, got himself a hot ar-tist."

Bear told me that he was heading out to his camp and that he could give me a lift to the store. I told him I was staying at my father's house so he said he'd drive me there.

We drive on up Main Street past Ricky's place. I look up at the windows. A light is flickering through a crack between the curtains I made. Ricky used to light candles when we wanted to make it extra special. Our candles, Ricky is burning our candles.

I'm screwing Bear James just as hard as I can. After we drove by Ricky's, Bear told me he had some good weed with him so we drove outside of town to Molly's Lake. We toked and looked out at the lake — it's just about all frozen now. And Bear told me he'll be dressing up as Santa this year for the curling club Christmas benefit, and something about the idea of Bear James being Santa Claus just cracked me up. Which is probably why I'm screwing him right now on the folded seats of his Rover. And it's going real good even though it's so cramped and weird because it's all happening so fast. Just minutes ago he was wearing this really cute embarrassed smile and he kept saying, "What's so funny about Santa?" And then wham, I go and kiss him and here I am, legs spread just about as wide as they can possibly go in a Rover. I'll say this about it, there sure is a lot of Bear James moving about in there. I sure am glad this didn't happen when I was still a kid.

We don't say much the whole way home. Just before we get to my father's street, Bear pulls over to the corner, and we sit there with the motor running.

"Well well well," he finally says, "who would have ever thought after all these years?"

"Really," I say, looking over at him. "So you do remember."

"Sure I remember," he says. "I was a regular asshole and you were what, fifteen?"

"Fourteen," I say.

"No wonder I tried to forget. But nothing ever, I mean we never ever, I would remember that."

"Oh, you just broke my heart, that's all." I laugh like he couldn't possibly have broken my heart. "That's why I couldn't understand how you could call me Miss Nancy. Remember? Miss Nancy?"

"Uh, no, I don't."

So I remind him. Miss Nancy was the name that Bear told me he was going to have painted on the boat he dreamed of owning. After we had driven around for an hour or so that day, we stopped to buy me a licorice ice-cream cone at Damrey's. Then all of a sudden he snapped his fingers and said he'd just remembered he had to go out to his uncle's camp to pick up a chain-saw. So we drove out of town and we sang all the way.

The camp looked like it was built out of old windows. There were round ones, diamond ones, even some stained-glass ones. There was even a big twelve-paned window in the ceiling. There were so many windows that being inside felt like being outside. I thought it was the neatest place in the world.

Since Bear was still my slave, I ordered him to let me stay a while. He said okay, but that was only because I was his master. We sat down on a bunk. I said I was getting cold. He put his arm around me and we leaned back on the bunk and he told me about this boat he wanted to own one day. I told him that I liked boats too, and that's when he told me that if he ever did get a boat, he was going to call it the *Miss Nancy.*

"I remember going out to the camp," he says now, as he turns on the defroster in the Rover, "and coming back, but was there more than that?"

I look at him quickly to see if he's joking.

On the way back to town that day I also kept looking over at Bear, who stared straight ahead at the road. My lips felt dry and stiff. Just twenty minutes before, in his uncle's cabin, he'd had his hands under my shirt. They felt so warm, just as if they belonged there. But then he trailed one hand down inside the front of my jeans and suddenly I felt as hot as the Tabasco sauce my cousin once dared me to taste. For once I was sorry my jeans were so tight. He seemed to be having such a hard time getting his fingers down there that I thought I should just reach down and unzip my fly. That's when he jumped away so quickly that I thought maybe I'd pinched his finger in the zipper.

"I must be nuts!" he said, pacing back and forth in front of me. He sounded a little out of breath when he said he had to get back to town or he'd be late for his job at the Co-op.

Most of the drive back to town I stared at the road too, trying to think of what I could say. At the end of my street he pulled the truck over to the curb and sighed. "You won't tell anybody about this, I hope."

"About what?" I said, a little worried.

He laughed and said, "That's my girl."

I opened the door of the truck and hopped out. "I guess I'll see you soon."

He said sure and drove off down the street. It was almost

dark. I felt cold and alone. I could tell my father wasn't home from work yet because there weren't any lights on in the house. The funny thing was that once I let myself in the door, I didn't know whether I should start singing or crying.

The next time I saw Bear James it was up at the rink. He was playing goalie for our junior team, the Scramblers. My friend Shawna and I cheered for him every time he stopped the puck. But when we were hanging around outside the rink afterwards and I stepped up to say hi, he walked right by me like I wasn't even there.

"You really don't remember?" I ask him now, as we park at that very same corner at the end of my father's street.

He looks at me and frowns. "I just remember driving out there with you, and bringing you back. How could I have broken your heart?"

"It's okay," I laugh, reaching for the door handle. "I think you made up for it tonight."

He asks if we can get together sometime soon. I say that I don't know, that I'll see.

I watch him drive away and I'm thinking, Holy fuck, what have I gone and done now?

I go into my father's house and right upstairs to have a bath. I just lie there as still as a branch in a frozen pond, except for the times I raise my leg to turn on the hot water tap with my toes. Whenever I think about Bear moving inside of me, I get this hot rush right up into my belly. But then I think of Ricky and the rush turns into a stone and my heart jumps like a caught fish. I haven't been with anyone but Ricky in all the time we've been together. Oh yeah? I tell myself. Well, now you're not with Ricky, remember?

Then my father knocks on the bathroom door and asks me if I'm okay. I tell him that I am just fine, that I am having a bath now so I won't tie up the bathroom in the morning. He tells me through the door that, in spite of my strange habits, it is nice to have me stay over. Then I hear his slippers flapping back down the hall, and that's when these hot tears start splashing into the water.

Alana is crouched under the store counter trying to set a mousetrap. She knows that Bear and I drove by Ricky's the other night and how we saw the candles behind the curtains, and I told her about this Rachel coming over with the paint and all. But that's it. Now I'm telling her that Ricky hasn't called in three days, and I guess my voice is starting to sound a little choky, because Alana stands right up and stares at me.
  "So why haven't you called him?"
  "I can't," I say.
  "You can't?"
  "No, I can't."
  "Well," she says, all frustrated, "if I thought Danny was doing someone else, I think I'd want to be one of the first to know. And you know why?"
  "Why?"
  "Because maybe I'd want to do someone else myself."
  Alana is getting suspicious. I can tell because she's starting to narrow her eyes every time Bear James comes into the store. He's been in twice since that night and both times I've pretty much ignored him.
  Alana says, "I guess you couldn't really blame Ricky if he was messing around, since every time he comes out here he sleeps on the couch. He is human, after all."
  "Oh thanks," I say, cracking a roll of quarters against the side of the counter. "That makes me feel so much better, especially after I followed your advice to not sleep with him till he quit drinking."
  "Well, didn't you say he hasn't had a drink in over a week? Isn't this what you want?"
  I don't answer Alana because I can't. Instead I go over to

the stove and poke at the fire.

Later in the day I'm sitting on the stool at the counter, watching the snow falling outside the window, and it's almost dusk. I see Danny heading back over the road from the farm. He stops by the side of the road to wait for a car to pass. I see Rachel's green Volvo drive by. Whoever is sitting beside her lifts a hand to Danny.

Danny comes into the store, whistling.

"That was Ricky, right?" I say, but my lips feel numb, like I've just been to the dentist.

"Yup," sighs Danny, going off to the washroom to wash his hands. "Wonder why they didn't stop."

I stare out the window. The knot in my stomach is starting to hurt real bad. They were headed in the direction of Rachel's schoolhouse. Rachel didn't even stop here at the store like she usually does. They didn't even look this way. Danny goes and puts more wood in the stove and stands there warming up his hands. He asks me if the Klinkhorns were in to pay their bill.

"No." I say, but it sounds more like a squeak.

"He's probably just going out there to paint or something."

"Or something," I whisper.

Alana and I are sitting in the car in the dark, just down the road from Rachel's schoolhouse. As soon as Alana came home from work she knew something was up. She looked over at Danny, who had just poured me some tea and he went right upstairs. I told Alana about seeing Ricky and Rachel drive by. She said, "So what are you going to do about it?"

"There's not much I can do, is there?"

She said, "Let's go for a drive."

Now I'm thinking I should just sneak up to the schoolhouse and look in a window. Alana thinks we should march on up and knock on the door, saying we were just driving around and thought we'd drop in.

"Oh yeah, and we'll say we always drive around in snowstorms for the fun of it," I say.

I crouch down and run to the schoolhouse. Snowflakes swirl around a window on the side. At first I don't see anything except all these dried fruits and flowers and herbs hanging from the ceiling. Then I spot Rachel standing over in a corner of the room. She has an easel in front of her and she's wearing a bright red blouse. I crane my neck to try to see what it is she could be painting. What I see is Ricky sitting across from her with an easel in front of him too. The difference, I notice, is that he isn't wearing his shirt. I watch him lift his brush up to the easel, and carefully stroke it down the canvas. High on his arm is a leather band I once gave him. All this time, his black eyes are looking hard at Rachel.

I'm alone in the trailer and crying my eyes out. A cold wind is somehow getting in through all my quilts. The window facing north keeps rattling. I keep asking myself how this could have happened. How stupid could I have been to think Ricky would wait around for me to decide if we'd ever be together again? Here I was, going around as if it was all up to me. This hit me on the way back from the schoolhouse. Alana kept asking me what I saw, was it really terrible, were they doing the deed? Nancy, what did you see already!? That's when I just burst out all over the place, which got Alana real upset because I don't know if she's ever seen me cry before. I wish I'd never left Ricky because I've just thrown away the very best part of my life.

Ricky shows up the next day. He and Rachel pull up to the pumps right before noon. Instead of going out there to pump the gas, I sit on my stool — I can't seem to move. Ricky sees me and waves. I manage to lift my hand. He gets out of the car and pumps the gas himself. Then he strolls right in like there's nothing wrong at all.

"Hi Nance," he says, and then he looks at my face. "What's wrong?"

He looks good. He looks rested and young. His hair is clean, and he's wearing a shirt I've never seen before. My heart is pounding like crazy, and I have to look away.

"Nance," he says, coming around behind the counter and making me look at him.

I push him away and say in my coldest voice, "I hate you."

The door clangs open and Rachel walks in. "Oh hi, Nancy, here's the money for the gas."

I take the money from her and ring it in. I stick my chin right up there like nothing in the world is wrong.

Ricky says to her, "I think I'll hang around here for a while, Rachel, but thanks for everything."

"Okay, you want your stuff?"

I watch them go out to the car and pull Ricky's knapsack and sleeping-bag out of the trunk.

I see Ricky laugh at something Rachel says and then wave to her as she pulls out onto the highway. I watch Danny coming across the road for lunch. He waves to her too. I'm thinking they all have some friggin' nerve.

The trailer is cold because I turned the stove way down when I went around to the store today. Ricky and I are warm enough, though, cuddled under my covers. We are just lying there, our bodies wrapped around each other as tightly as Alana's braid. I look at the clock above the stove. Soon I'll have to get back to the store so Danny can get back to the dairy.

When Danny told me and Ricky to get lost, we tried to

go for a walk down to the beach. We got past the orchard but we found snow had drifted over the road in the night. So we went back to my trailer and I sat on the bed with my arms around my knees and he sat in the chair and made me tell him what it was that was killing me. Then he told me right out that nothing had happened with Rachel. He said they painted for a while and then he slept in his sleeping-bag on a spare mattress. I asked him whose shirt he was wearing. He looked down at it and said that it was Rachel's, that he had slopped some paint on his. Then he told me he loved me. His face looked almost as scared as mine must have looked last night when I thought he was gone.

"You really like her? Rachel?" I say, with my face burrowed against his neck.

"You know what I like about her the most?" he says. "Maybe this sounds stupid, but when I'm around her I really feel as if I'm an artist."

"So?" I say, lifting my head to look at him. "I've been telling you that for years. Now all of a sudden it takes some stranger to tell you what you are?"

He holds me tighter. "She doesn't have to tell me. It's like she just believes it so I guess that makes me believe it too."

I can't help it. It's all very nice that Ricky has found a friend who believes in him, but this kind of talk starts pissing me off so I go and say, "And I suppose a little candlelight helps with all this accepting stuff too."

Ricky looks down at me. "What are you talking about?"

"I'm talking about two in the other goddamn morning when I was driving by and you had the candles burning," I say, turning away from him to look out the window.

"You were driving by at two in the morning?"

Then of course I have to tell him about going to the Purple Hall, and of course he asks me who I was with when

I saw the candles, so it comes out that it was Bear. I'm quick to tell him that Bear drove me straight to my father's house, but then I go and yawn.

"Good for Bear," says Ricky, pulling away just a little, enough that it feels like there's a sudden draft between us. "Always in the right place at the right time."

Bear James is a hero. Here it is, just two weeks before Christmas, and he goes and saves old Pogey Chapman's life. Pogey had a heart attack and fell in the snow in the park. Bear was just coming from the curling club Christmas benefit and he was still wearing the Santa suit. He came across Pogey lying there in the snow and he did CPR on him right away. I guess, when Pogey came around, he rubbed his eyes and shook his head and said, "What d'ya think of that, I just got kissed by Santa!"

The word went around fast and it was written up in the paper. I went into town one day to visit my father and even he smiled when he read the story, and said if there was ever a time when this old town needed a little miracle to perk it up, it was now. I thought that was awful big of him since if there's one thing he hates in this world it's a drunk. And Pogey Chapman is one of the worst. Still, I guess Pogey learned a bit of a lesson out of all this, because he started going to AA meetings over in the next town and was quoted in the paper as saying, "It's not every day you get saved by Santa. I figure that's the next best thing to being saved by God himself."

Now we're having a party here at the store. Everybody keeps pouring Bear a drink, since he's a hero. He's getting hammered and he's not alone. I'm into the rum and Alana is too. There's a tree over by the window, complete with blinking lights to match the ones outside over the door. Danny and I moved the shelves to one side so there would be room for dancing. I asked Ricky to come out to the party but he said he didn't think he should because of all the drinking. He wondered if I wanted to come into town to stay with him and maybe play a little chess but, like I told him, it's my party too so it would look pretty rude of me not to be there.

Alana went and invited Rachel to the party as well. I've talked to Rachel a few times since she had Ricky out at her schoolhouse. I have to admit I can see what Ricky sees in her, besides her long black hair and her big brown eyes, that is. I think it's the way she gives you all of her attention when you talk. She acts as though whatever you say is important. I don't know if she actually did the deed with Ricky or not, but I know I sure would want to if I was staring at Ricky Chase and he had no shirt on. I even saw that painting one day, when Alana and I were back-road driving and we stopped in at the schoolhouse. Alana went right ahead and told Rachel that we knew about them painting out here that night. Rachel just said, "Oh, let me show you. We did some wonderful work that night." I just bet you did, I thought, but I had to admit the painting of Ricky was really good. It showed the strong lines of his arms and chest, all right, but what got to me was that she caught the look he gets on his face when he paints. As I stand there looking at it, I realize it's the same look he gets when he loves.

Some more people from town arrive at the party. One car brings Shell and Katrina and even Eddie. Katrina has this great voice and her Eddie brings in his fiddle. Even the older locals who were invited, who have been mostly standing around the counter all evening, start clapping and singing. Alana's just sitting back on the couch, her hair down, loose and wild, her hands slapping her knees. I sit beside her. She's started telling me something about the Christmas party at the hotel when I look over and see Bear staring at me. He gives me this little nod before I turn away. Alana catches it.

She says, "I heard something at the party today that you might be interested in."

"What's that?" I say.

She folds her arms across her chest, "I heard that you and Bear were parked out at Molly's Lake that night you went to town."

"So?" I say, yawning. "We went out to smoke a joint."

"Yeah? That's not what I heard."

"Well, what exactly did you hear then, Alana?"

"The point is, me dear," she says, "the person who told me has, you can be sure, told Ricky."

"Tripper O'Leery?" I say. "Nobody believes anything he says."

"Oh no?" she says. "It seems he saw Bear's Rover rocking all over the place."

"Oh fuck," I say.

"You mean it's really true?" says Alana, and when I finally look at her she bursts out laughing. "Get out of town, you and Bear James? In the Rover?" And then she goes off, leaves me just like that, still laughing.

And here I thought she'd be all pissed off that I hadn't told her.

Most of the locals left long ago, so the pot comes out, which gets some people going crazy with dancing and laughing while others get right quiet. I watch Alana as she gets dreamy-eyed looking at something on the other side of the room. I look over and I see that it's Bear she's watching. I look at Danny, who has been dancing a lot with Katrina. He's watching Alana. He leaves Katrina right in the middle of a dance, but she doesn't seem to notice as she goes floating past the cereal boxes and canned peas. Danny stands behind Alana and slips his arms around her waist. He starts kissing the back of her neck. She leans back into him and it takes them all of about two minutes to disappear upstairs. I've seen them go off with each other like this a thousand times over the years, but all this time I thought they only had each other on their minds.

I'm in the back store-room with Bear James. I was just reaching for another beer out of the cooler when he whispered in my ear that he wanted to go somewhere with me to smoke a joint. I asked him why we couldn't just smoke it there in the party. Then he told me that he wanted to talk to me, so here we are.

"Good party, eh?" he says, handing me the joint.

"Yeah, not bad," I say, taking a deep haul off it. It's cold out here in the porch so I stomp my feet to keep them warm.

"So?" he says.

"So what?"

"You're not talking to me."

"I hadn't noticed," I say, looking around the room. "Hey, you're a real hero now, aren't you, Bear?"

He blows a stream of smoke up to the ceiling, and says, "You know, I've been trying to remember back to when we drove out to the camp that time. Jesus, it was so long ago. Are you sure I didn't, you know, try anything with you out there? Because if I did — well shit, I didn't, did I?"

I look at him. His face is turning bright red and he looks so freaked out that I have to turn around and face the sacks of dogfood leaning against the wall so he won't see me laugh. Because it's not funny, but it is. This pot is stronger than his homegrown. I wonder where he got it. I should say something to him, like he wasn't the only one in the cabin that day, that sure I was young but I was pretty hot for the likes of Bear James back then. Yessiree, I was.

"Nancy?" I hear him say. Or rather, he sounds as if he's choking. I fold my arms across my chest and turn.

"Why didn't you speak to me after that? That's all I want

to know."

Bear sits on a crate marked McCormick's Apple Juice and, picking a beer cap up off the floor, says, "What if I tell you I'm sorry?"

"Not enough,"

"Okay, what if I tell you that the reason I never spoke to you again was simply because you were still a little kid?"

"You didn't think that out at the camp," I say, staring down at him while he fiddles with the beer cap.

"Okay," he says slowly, "how about if I tell you that your father convinced me to never even so much as look in your direction, at least until you were such an age as to — how old are you now, anyway, twenty-six? Twenty-seven?"

"My father? What does he have to do with anything?"

"He must have followed us all the way out to the camp and back. I saw him in the rear-view mirror just after I let you off at your street. He started following me all through town. I'm telling you, it was fucking strange, like he was some kind of ghost. He made me so nervous I drove right off Bridge Street into a signpost. But when I looked around for him, he was gone. I could have been killed, for Christ's sake, and he just drove off. And you wonder why I never spoke to you again? Christ Almighty, it's a wonder old Rick is still walking around."

I sit down on the bags of potatoes in the corner. Maybe it's the dope, maybe it's the rum — whatever it is, I'm getting dizzy. I keep seeing Ricky's hand all bandaged up that day after he was hauled into jail, and I'm wondering what else my father may have done or said to him over the years. I get this weird thought that this must be what it's like to find out you're adopted or something.

"Thank God we're adults now," Bear is saying, as he sits down beside me. He laughs. "Or should I say thank God your old man finally retired?"

GETTING OUT OF TOWN

I stand up and look at him sitting there with his feet spread apart on the floor and his face all ruddy from the booze, and I start laughing on my way to the door. I turn around to say, "You know what, Brendon James, you really do look like Santa Claus."

Rachel has just been telling me all about the west coast. She was saying that in Vancouver the seasons blend into each other. I think I just mumbled something about not being able to imagine surprises in the weather.

Back at the party I was starting to feel all queasy so I went and put on my jacket. Outside the air felt cold and good. Then the door opened behind me and Rachel stepped out, pulling that long bright coat of hers closed. We started walking towards the beach without saying a word. There was a big windstorm the other day that blew the snow right off the fields and drifted it into the ditches. The moon is bright and high in the sky. The snow looks right blue in the night light. It's so quiet that I can hear a car slowing on the highway. A door slams and the car keeps going down the road. I listen until the sound disappears.

Now we're almost at the beach and she asks me what's wrong and I just go and tell her. I can't believe I'm doing it, either. I hardly know her but here I am, telling her how all this time I thought the drinking was the big problem between Ricky and me, but now I only see that as part of a much bigger problem. I tell her I feel like I don't know which way I'm facing any more.

"Sounds to me like all you want is some control of your own life," Rachel says.

"I thought I was in control when I moved out here last month, but all I have is one big mess."

We've reached the beach, and the quiet surrounds us like fog. Ridged ice floes have piled up onto the sand and stretch out into the water. We walk to the edge, where tiny waves are lapping the bare sand like a whole lot of little kisses. It's a tame night out on the strait. Rachel is going on about how pink the ice seems to be in the moonlight. I tell her that's because the floes are loaded with red sand. In the daytime they look orange.

She tells me she's going back to Vancouver in the spring to teach some art courses. I feel I should be happy about that, because it means I won't have to worry about her and Ricky any more, but I feel sad too, like I'm going to lose someone important. And here I hardly know her.

"But you have to stay for the summer," I hear myself say. "It's so beautiful here in the summer."

"It's beautiful now," she says, looking over the ice floes. "It looks like a moonscape almost."

"Looks more like a graveyard to me," I say, taking in a deep breath and blowing it back out towards the sky.

"Did you ever think of leaving here?"

"Leave?" I say. "Once I thought I might take a forestry course down in Truro, but I didn't."

"Why not?"

"Because I couldn't see me being anywhere else but here," I say, but as soon as I do I have this picture of me in my head. I'm walking somewhere, maybe on a city street, maybe it's the forest. Wherever it is, there are tall things around me and I am all alone.

When we first open the door to the store it looks like just about everybody has left the party. The tape player is turned off and the candles have been blown out, except for one on a table near the couch.

"I guess I should be going home," says Rachel, but then all of a sudden we hear Bear's voice from over by the couch.

"Wait a minute, Rachel," he says, "I need a lift home."

GETTING OUT OF TOWN

We go over to where Bear sits across from Ricky on the floor. Their heads are bent over my chess board. Ricky must have brought it with him. I ask him how he got out here, but he acts like he doesn't hear or see me. He's drunk, I can tell that right away. I can also see that the game looks pretty evenly matched, even though Ricky has just taken a rook.

"You didn't tell me Bear was a chess player, Nance," Ricky says to me, setting down his rum bottle and wiping his chin with the back of his hand. "You were very naughty, Nancy." He wags his finger at me. "Naughty Nancy, that's what I'm going to call you from now on."

"I didn't know he could play," I say.

"Oh, he's a good player all right," Ricky is saying, staring again at the board. "Hey, he may even be good enough, eh Nance?"

"What do you mean, good enough? Good enough for what?" asks Rachel, who has sat down on the couch and rested her elbows on her knees. I can tell she hasn't a clue what's going on here.

"Let me tell you what's good about all this," Ricky says slowly, like he's telling a two-year-old. "It all has to do with Nancy here. She's having a hard time deciding what the fuck she's doing and we're trying to help her out, right, Bear?"

Bear lets his breath out in a low whistle and says, "To tell you the truth, buddy, I thought we were just playing chess. But if you say we're helping Nancy make a decision, then I guess that's okay with me too."

I stand there in my boots, in the warmth of the stove, and I start shaking. Ricky doesn't even look up at me but just stares at the board. Bear looks like he'd rather be anywhere else. Rachel looks at me with a question in her eyes.

I turn around and run. I run out the door and I run back down the road towards the beach. My boots pound the snow, my breathing comes out hard and loud. I raise my arms to the sides and I run like that, like I'm flying. I'm flying right the fuck out of here. Before I reach the beach something comes tearing out of me. It's a howl and it's a laugh. It's the same cry you sometimes hear around town on a Friday night, when everybody figures they've just been set free.

THE SCRAG AND THE CHESS SET

Rena Dickson opens the door to Chase's poolroom and walks in through a dusty hall. When she and Angel step into the room, the boys look up from the tables. Over by the windows, Ricky pushes a broom. Rena gets an orange pop from the machine and, tipping the bottle up to her lips, gulps it down in one thirsty swig. She wipes her mouth and smiles at Ricky.

Rena Dickson is the only female who ever comes into Chase's, unless you count Angel, who is black and white and always scratching her fleas. Rena found her one day at the beach when she'd been out there at a cottage with some tourist from Saskatoon. Before she hitch-hiked back to town the next morning, she thought she'd go down to the beach since it was something she hardly ever got to do. She heard the cry before she saw the burlap bag that had been washed up next to a big red rock. In it were three drowned puppies and Angel. Rena pulled Angel out from the mess and Angel has been following her around ever since.

"How's it going, Rena?" says Ricky, pushing a path through the cigarette butts and dustballs that speckle the red and white tiles.

"Not bad," says Rena. Yesterday she heard a rumour that

Nancy has left Ricky, left town. She wonders if it's true.

"Hi, little Angel," Ricky says, squatting down to ruffle Angel's ears. She licks at his hand and her tail thumps on the dusty floor.

At one table, the Bishop brothers and Tripper O'Leery play eight ball. Tripper suddenly shouts, "Shee-it." The three ball is way out of reach and the only bridge in the place got broken yesterday. He looks at Rena and says, so everyone can hear, "Hey Rena, I need something long and skinny with a couple of bumps on it. Mind lying on the table and taking off your top?"

"Ha ha, very funny," says Rena, shaking her bangs out of her face and smiling around at all the boys.

Then Father Jack comes over to her and says, "Come over here, Rena, I want to talk to you."

"What about?"

"Never mind, just come," says Father Jack.

Rena goes with him over to one of the dirty windows that nobody could ever hope to see through. They look at it anyway, and Jack tells her that he's having a poker game that night and she should come if she wants.

She says, "Yeah, okay, maybe." Then she wanders over to the counter, where Ricky sits drawing something. She looks at the paper in front of him and tries to figure out why he would want to draw a picture of the ceiling. He has also drawn the lightbulb that hangs down from a dusty cord. Pink insulation spills out around the mouldings on the ceiling. Ricky puts down his pencil.

"Get you something, Rena?"

"I just, I just wondered if you could keep Angel here for a while. I have to meet Mom at the bus terminal," says Rena, her voice catching like it always seems to do when she's around him.

"No problem," Ricky says, opening the door beside the

counter. Angel settles down at his feet and lays her chin on his shoe.

Rena leans against the wall and, looking down at her fingers, says, "I heard Nancy went out west."

Ricky pops the top off a pop bottle and flicks it into the garbage. "Vancouver."

"That's far. I've never been farther away than Moncton."

"Vancouver is just about as far as you can get. Some people move to the next town to get away. Nancy had to move to the next ocean."

Rena doesn't know what to say. Even when she was a kid she never quite knew what to say to Ricky Chase. He hung around with her brother Perry quite a bit in those days. Perry acted like a big shot, telling her to buzz off, but Ricky always asked about Spark and Flo, her pet muskrats.

"Maybe Nancy will come back," Rena says.

"Maybe," says Ricky, getting up from his chair, and reaching into his pocket. He pulls out a ten-dollar bill. "Give this to Dottie for me. She lent it to me the other night."

At the Terminal Diner, Rena sits on a stool and waits for the bus. Her mother visits Rena's brother on Fridays. Tomorrow it will be Rena's turn to hitch-hike down to the pen. Perry used to own an auto shop, but he started selling stolen car parts on the side. Now he's in for two years.

The bus pulls in, and through the window Rena sees Dottie step off. She wears a scarf over her frizzy hair and carries the brown purse Rena gave her one Christmas.

"So?" says Rena, when Dottie has joined her at the counter and they've ordered two hot roast-beef sandwiches.

"So here he is due for a parole hearing, and what's he been doing?" says Dottie, rubbing her forehead. "Been going around with a bunch of drug dealers in there, like that Tyler King."

"There's no crime in just hanging around with someone, is there?"

"Oh yeah? Well, you're just as stupid as your brother if you think that there parole board won't hear about it." Dottie slaps her hand on the counter. The two waitresses look up quickly, and then start snickering beside the coffee machine.

Rena hunches her shoulders and whispers, "You don't know, anything can happen."

"Just like Perry could go gettin' himself more time too." Dottie drags on her cigarette. Rena watches her mother's cheeks suck in and the lines above her mouth deepen. When she wipes at her eyes, Rena hands her a napkin. Dottie pushes it away. "It's just smoke in my eye, for Christ's sake. You want the whole friggin' world to think I'm crying?"

They stare out the window. Across the street they see Jennifer Sullivan going into the Golden Locks Beauty Salon. Rena knew her in school, but Jennifer was on the student council and didn't have much use for Rena. Tomorrow Jennifer will be marrying Cameron McLeod, the mayor's son. Rena always thought he was cute but she never really knew him either.

"It'll be a big fat fancy wedding, won't it now?" her mother is saying. "All them mucky-mucks showin' off their cars and their clothes. Now just think if you was marryin' that Cameron McLeod."

Rena says, "You know Ricky's girlfriend left town?"

Dottie nods. "That Nancy McKinnon reminded me of her mother, colder than charity, that one. Always thought she was too good for this town."

"I heard Nancy left because of the drinking," Rena says, and goes back to looking out the window. "It's not like Ricky's a mean drunk. I just don't know how anybody could leave somebody like Ricky."

Dottie turns from the window to stare at Rena. "Ricky

THE SCRAG AND THE CHESS SET

Chase is part Indian. I don't want no daughter of mine goin' with no Indian."

"That reminds me," says Rena. "He gave me ten dollars to give to you."

"Oh, for the pizza," says Dottie, turning away to tuck the bill into her purse.

A soft spring evening has settled over town as Rena heads back to the poolroom. The sun on the sandstone buildings makes them look pinker than their daytime red. She wonders why Father Jack asked her to come over tonight. Mind you, ever since his wife left him, it doesn't take much for him to party, just like it doesn't take much for Rena to hang around at Jack's either, seeing as the boys all go there. But still, this is the first time he has actually asked her.

When she stops by the poolroom, Ricky is hauling the vacuum cleaner out of the bathroom. He starts it up and runs the brush over the tops of the tables. Rena looks around the room. The evening sun has found its way in through the windows. Gold rays slice through the dusty air to the other wall, where Ricky's drawings are all pinned up with thumbtacks. Rena goes over and looks at them, smoothing out their curling edges with her hands. She sees one picture — no, two — of Tripper, and there's one of Father Jack chalking up. Ricky even drew one of his grandfather who opened this poolroom sometime soon after the First World War. Dottie said he was a good old geezer, drunk as all get out, but she said you never saw anyone so crazy about a woman, and here she was a Micmac Indian who wouldn't even marry him. There's a story that he walked the nine miles from town to the junction where she was having his baby down there in the shack where she lived. And all this while a winter storm was sweeping on up the bay.

Rena says, "Hey Ricky, do you want me to clean the

bathroom for you? I don't mind, since you kept Angel and all."

Ricky smiles at Rena. "Just think of it as a favour to Dottie for lending me the money."

"Oh, okay, thanks," Rena says, looking down at Angel, who thumps her tail on the floor. "You think you'll be going down to Father Jack's later, Ricky?"

"You never know," says Ricky, snapping down the light switches. "I'll see you around, okay?"

"Okay, bye," Rena says. She leaves the poolroom with Angel and heads on home to take a bath.

It's some kind of a stag party for Cameron McLeod. Rena realizes that when she steps into Jack's kitchen. Already they're playing poker. Tripper O'Leery takes up one whole end of the table. Cameron and Jack sit on one side and the Bishop brothers on the other. They all ignore her except Jack, who says, "Get me a beer, will ya, Rena?"

After Rena passes out the beer she goes into the bathroom and pushes her hair up into a ponytail. Someone bangs on the door and tells her to hurry up. She looks in the mirror and puts on some pink lipstick. She smiles to see if it helps hide her front teeth. It never does but she hopes the lipstick will stick out the most. She pulls back her shoulders and goes out to the kitchen.

Ricky has just rolled in through the back door and is sitting at a corner of the table. Rena can tell he has already been into the booze because his eyelids get all droopy when he drinks. She watches the game and brings more beer to the table. When Jack opens the rum, she gets down glasses. All the while she hums to herself.

The boys are having a good old time. Cameron McLeod is looking right at home here in Father Jack's kitchen, now that he's all drunked up. Tripper is teasing him about getting married. "Here it is your last night a free man and what are you doing about it? Hey, where's the girl who comes out of the cake?" He grabs Rena by the waist and pulls her down into his lap. She giggles and tries to get up.

Tripper says, "Here, Cam, take Rena. She may not come out of a cake but she tastes some good."

"That may well be," laughs Cameron, "but I'm not that drunk, yet."

Rena's cheeks turn red, but she laughs along with all the boys anyway. She looks at Ricky, who is only staring at his cards and doesn't seem to be paying any attention to what's going on. Once, when she was really drunk at a party and Ricky was there, Tripper shoved him into a bedroom with her. She tried her best to get him to just sit beside her, but all he did was lean against the door and talk to her about her job at the dry-cleaners.

Tripper is saying, "Hey, don't worry, Rena. Old Cam's just afraid of what you might do to him."

Cameron laughs. "It's not her I'm afraid of, it's Jennifer."

Rena sits on Father Jack's bed. She's wearing a T-shirt that she found on the floor. A purple candle burns on the dresser. The Bishop brothers have been in to see her. While one is busy doing it to her, the other likes to tell him where to poke it next. They all laugh about it, because ever since they were kids they've been playing the same game.

Rena doesn't tell anybody anything about who she does it with, like the fact that Tripper can never get it up. All he ends up doing is laying his head against her chest. He told her once that the only thing in this world he loves is her tits. She believes him, because she's never known him to love anything else.

Father Jack has been in to see her too. Except that he didn't really look at her and hardly touched her either. He just pulled down his zipper and pointed. Once, when she looked up at him, he reached down and tugged at her ponytail, holding onto it tightly until she heard him suck in his breath and mutter something between his teeth.

Now Rena carefully spreads polish on her nails and listens to them out there in the kitchen. Cameron is saying, "Give me one good reason why I should screw that scrag."

"Be-cause," she hears Jack say, "she'll give you a ride you won't forget till you're good and dead."

"Yeah, and who the hell knows what I'd catch from her either?" Cameron says, but he's laughing when he says it. Rena knows he'll be coming in. She puts away her polish and hears Jack say, "Then just ask her for a blow job, for Christ's sake."

Cameron comes in a minute later, looking right shy. He blows out the candle and stands there in the dark. The first thing he says is "I didn't mean what I said earlier."

Rena scuffs her feet along Main Street. It's two in the morning and starting to rain. Nighthawks call out as they flit through dark trees. She left Father Jack's soon after Cameron's Jennifer came storming in looking for him. Lucky for Cameron he'd just left Rena and gone back into the kitchen. But when Jennifer saw Rena come into the room, she let Cameron have it. Cameron grabbed his jacket and took off out the back door with Jennifer behind him crying, "Were you with that scrag?" Rena and the boys couldn't stop laughing because they could hear her shouting all the way down the street, "You'd better be telling me the truth, Cameron McLeod!"

The game broke up after that, and when Rena asked Tripper what had happened to Ricky, Tripper told her that the little son of a squaw had gone to jerk off for all he knew.

THE SCRAG AND THE CHESS SET

Rena stops and looks across the street at the dark windows above the Jupiter Restaurant, where Ricky lives. She turns to walk away, but she hears a small noise coming from the doorway of the Baptist church. She squints her eyes and sees Ricky crouched in there on the step. He waves a bottle at her, and then takes a drink. Rena takes the bottle from him. She drinks from it even though she doesn't like rum all that much. They sit and watch the rain.

"So, how's old Perry doing anyway?" Ricky finally says. "He must be up for parole soon."

"Next month," Rena says, wrapping her arms around her knees. "It's his birthday tomorrow and I don't have a present for him. Even if I had the money, I still wouldn't know what to get."

The rain running off the overhang above their heads is almost like a waterfall now. Ricky suddenly snorts and Rena says, "What?"

"I was just thinking you could start charging those guys something. I knew a lady in Halifax who made a bundle doing exactly what you do."

Rena stares out at the street. The raindrops bounce off the pavement like white jewels. Suddenly she jumps up from the step, knocking Ricky hard against the stone wall. The bottle drops and breaks. Rena runs out through the rain.

"Hey, Rena!" she hears him call, and when she looks back she sees him weaving up the middle of the street. He is waving his arms and is shouting something she can't quite hear.

A car comes around the corner, fast, and charges down the street towards Ricky. Rena shouts and waves her arms but the car keeps going and Ricky is still in the street. She covers her eyes with her hands, and hears the scream of squealing tires. When she opens her eyes, the car is purring along beside her and Ricky has stumbled onto the sidewalk. The driver is just a drunk kid and so are his friends. He asks her if she needs a lift. She shakes her head and the kid says, "Aw come on, Rena." She points to Ricky, who has now fallen onto a bench, and the car squeals off up the street.

Rena pushes Ricky up the stairs into his place. She has never been here before. They must have knocked some of the walls down to make the room so big. At one end, a painting sits on a newspaper covering the bright blue floor. It's Nancy, Rena can see that right away. She looks at the pale face and staring eyes.

She says, "You are some good artist, Ricky."

Ricky laughs. "You think so, do you, Rena?"

"Yeah I do," she says, looking around at the walls. It's almost like having the whole town inside the room. There's a painting of the big old Parker house that burned down last year. There's the church across the street and the doorway they've just been sitting in. Then she sees a painting of the salt marshes creeping up to the edge of town. In the background there's a dike that holds back the tide, and right up in front are the tall green grasses, bent over like there's some wind under those low black clouds.

Rena nods at it. "Perry used to let me come with him to check his muskrat traps out there on the marsh."

"Hey, didn't you have two of them as pets?"

"You mean Spark and Flo?"

"Yeah, Spark and Flo. You kept them for a long time, didn't you?"

"Except for when Perry needed some cash," Rena laughs. "But he always got me two more babies to make up for them. And I always called them Spark and Flo."

She's about to tell him how she'd look out the kitchen window and see the two pelts tacked to the shed door, but she looks at Ricky and thinks he's frowning.

"Don't think bad of Perry, Ricky. Even in prison he's

THE SCRAG AND THE CHESS SET

always worrying about me."

"I know that, Rena."

It's quiet in the room except for the noise from down on the street.

"Those are nice curtains," she says.

"You know what?" Ricky finally says. "Maybe I have something you can give to Perry for his birthday."

He sits down on the couch in the middle of the room, and reaches under it. Pulling out a box, he puts it on the middle cushion. Rena sits on the other side. "What is it?"

"Chess set," Ricky says, opening the box. Several pieces fall onto the couch.

"Is it easy to play?" she asks, reaching between the cushions to find a piece. "I don't know if Perry can play this."

"Everybody plays in there. Somebody'll teach him."

Rena picks up a piece. "But I couldn't pay you for it, unless maybe...." She laughs and flicks her bangs out of her eyes. "You know."

"Oh, Rena." He shakes his head. "I only said that before because I figured, if you're going to let them use you like that, then why not make them pay?"

Rena sticks her chin up and says, "You mean like you paid Dottie? That what you mean?"

Ricky puts his thumbs up to his forehead and rubs it. Rena realizes he's laughing.

"What's so fuckin' funny?" she says.

"Nothing. To tell you the truth, I didn't know she charged."

"Maybe not to people she really likes," she says, raising her eyebrows.

"Who, me?" He laughs. "No, not me. And don't go changing the subject. We're talking about you. Why do you feel you have to screw every man in town?"

"Jesus, Ricky," Rena says, feeling her face get hot.

"Jesus?"

"No, not Jesus." She swats him on the shoulder. "I'm just not used to talking about it, that's all."

She looks away, looks out at the blinking sign of the Jupiter Restaurant. When she looks back at Ricky he has closed his eyes and is resting back against the couch.

"Maybe I just like being with the boys, maybe that's all there is to it."

"They treat you like garbage and you like being with them?"

Rena looks down at the floor and picks up another chess piece lying there by her foot. "So? You treated Nancy like a friggin' queen, and she threw you away like garbage."

He opens his eyes. She watches him as he walks over to the painting of Nancy on the floor. He taps at the bottom of the frame with the toe of his boot.

"Ricky?" Rena says, as softly as she can. "Ricky?"

When he doesn't answer she says, "This game, chess? Can you teach me it?"

Just after dawn, Rena steps out onto the street. Now she knows the names of all the chess pieces and what they can do. Ricky ended up falling asleep there on the couch while she was trying to remember how it was that the knight was supposed to move. After she put the pieces back into the box, she almost reached over to touch him, because she knows how easy a sleeping man can be — especially one with such a heavy heart. She stared at the chess set sitting there in her lap and decided she wouldn't take it to Perry after all. Instead she slid it back under the couch. Then she covered Ricky with a knitted blanket that was lying on the floor nearby.

The sun is coming up. It slices between the buildings, striking a red gash upon the sandstone church across the street. In a few hours the big wedding will be taking place, and the

THE SCRAG AND THE CHESS SET

bells will be ringing all over town. Rena swings her arms as she walks down towards the marsh. Angel will be waiting at home for her, wanting her breakfast by now. When Rena tied her up last night she whined and barked, and Rena could hear her all the way uptown.

BECAUSE OF THE TIME CHANGE

"Tripper O'Leery isn't dead after all," my father said when he greeted me at the airport. It must have been because I'd been gone so long, I think he hardly knew what else to say. I tucked my arm through his as we walked to his car.

He told me more about Tripper on the drive home. It was the first I'd heard of it — Tripper being dead in the first place, and how all of a sudden he was alive again. I guess the rumour got started when somebody saw him heading out onto the marshes with a gun a few days ago. My father added that he'd heard someone say Tripper had been acting very strange lately, saying things about disappearing for ever. And then just when everybody was getting used to the idea that he had really gone and done it, here he'd shown up yesterday, walking through town as though he'd never left.

"The thing is, he won't say what it was he was up to out there with the gun," my father said, as he fumbled between the seats looking for his sunglasses.

"I guess it could have been ducks," I said, finding them for him.

"Not with a .22," he said. "No, I figure he was just drunk and went out there to shoot at a few muskrats."

The first chance I got, after visiting with my father, I went out to the Four Reasons Stop to visit Alana. She and Danny were the same as ever, except for Danny losing his hair. As soon as he saw me, he took his cap off.

"There," he said, "you've seen it. Alana's always saying the reason I wear a cap is to hide it."

Alana laughed. "And you'd best stop wearing the thing, seeing as every time you take it off, you lose a few more."

"That's okay, Danny," I said, "you have way more hair than my husband does, and I still love him."

Alana looks pretty much the same as when I last saw her, but that was only two years ago, when I gave birth to Rachel. Alana flew all the way to Vancouver to help me out for a week. It was while she was there that I noticed her accent. And all this time I'd thought it was just Newfies and Islanders who had them. But hearing Alana made me ask Elliot if he'd ever noticed that I had an accent. He laughed and told me that, when he first met me, he thought I was putting it on. He said he once almost called me a hick during a fight, but was afraid of how I might react. I told him it was a good thing he was a sensible man because otherwise we never would have ended up having Rachel.

Then Danny asked me if I'd heard about Tripper O'Leery.

"He sure got us good, going off and pretending to kill himself so everybody'd feel guilty for hating him."

"Oh, come on," Alana said, "don't give him credit for working all that out himself. He just took off to the marsh with a gun because he was drunk and stupid. Then he probably passed out. I can't stand how everybody's making it out to be such a mystery."

Danny laughed and said to me, "You see? A lot of good it did him to pull off a disappearing act. Now that Alana knows he's okay, she can go back to hating him. But you should have seen her crying her eyes out yesterday when she thought he was dead."

"Well, he is someone we know, after all," said Alana, looking up from her tea.

I guess if anyone had a reason to hate Tripper O'Leery, besides me of course, it would be Alana. Once, when her daughter, Kim, was taking a shower, Alana came around the side of the house in time to see Tripper peeking in through the bathroom window. All she did was tell him that if he ever set foot near her place again she'd tell Danny, and that Danny would be sure to kill him. He tried to deny the whole thing, of course, said he was so drunk he thought it was the kitchen window he'd been looking through, just to see if we were in there. After he'd slunk off down the road to hitchhike back to town, I told Alana she really should tell Danny. At least that would be the end of Tripper coming round and taking Ricky off on drunks that could last a whole week.

A car drove up to the pumps outside and, while Danny was out filling it up, I went and asked Alana about Ricky. I'd heard that he was living with Rena Dickson and they'd just had a baby. Alana has kept me up to date even though I don't really think about Ricky much any more. Elliot and I have been married for five solid years. We know people who come from all over the world. On weekends we go skiing on mountains so white it sometimes hurts my eyes just looking at them. And now we have Rachel. Soon she'll come skiing with us too.

Now Alana was telling me that ever since Ricky's baby was born, he hardly ever drinks.

"I wonder how long that will last," I said.

"And you should see the baby," she said. "You look in her eyes and you could be looking straight at Ricky."

"Really?" I said, looking at the teapot on the wood stove.

"Think you're going to see him while you're home?" she

asked, as she got up to pour more tea into my cup.

"Who? Ricky?" I said, yawning because of the time change. "Not unless I run into him."

"Well, that's not very likely," Alana said. "Nobody sees much of him any more, not even Tripper O'Leery."

Once, when Ricky and I were out walking, I started going on about Tripper this and Tripper that and Ricky stopped suddenly and looked at me. "You ever wonder why nobody can stand Tripper?"

I said, "Because he's an asshole?"

"Besides that." Ricky laughed and squeezed my shoulder. "It's because he isn't afraid to say the truth."

"You mean like those things he says about me?"

"What things?"

"You know, that I'm this little mouse who's so afraid of my own shadow I don't dare move?"

Ricky shrugged. "All I'm saying is that if Tripper believes something to be true, then I guess it's his choice whether or not to say it."

"But do you think it's true? What he says about me?"

"Of course not," Ricky says, squeezing my hand. "But the difference is I love you."

I couldn't talk to him for the rest of the night. It was as if he'd forgotten what Tripper'd said just the week before. We were at a party and just standing around in the kitchen when Tripper suddenly shivered. Somebody said, "What's wrong, Tripper, somebody step on your grave?" He said, "I don't know, I feel like I'm standing next to an ice-cube or something." Then he jumped as if he hadn't known I was there all along and said, "Oh, it's only little Mousey McKinnon! Jesus girl, let me warm you up." He wrapped his entire self around me and I just about gagged before I pushed him away. Everybody was laughing at all this, of course, and when I looked

BECAUSE OF THE TIME CHANGE

at Ricky he turned away some quick, but not so quick that I couldn't see he was laughing too. Tripper, I could tell, was lapping this all up.

In fact I think it was the happiest day of Tripper's life when I left Ricky for good. But I don't think he was counting on Rena Dickson moving in so fast to take my place. Mind you, I was surprised too. I knew Ricky always had a soft spot for Rena, but Rena's a slut, and I mean a real slut. She'd have to be to do it with Tripper O'Leery.

The whole reason for me coming home last week was because my father decided to marry a woman he's been sneaking around with for years. I always thought it was right romantic the way they acted in public like casual friends. Of course everybody knew, but still nobody could say for sure. They must have finally gotten tired of playing the game, because yesterday they got married right out on my father's front veranda. By the time they got the rings on their fingers, there were cars parked on both sides of the street. People who'd just been driving by screeched to a stop when they saw big Leftie McKinnon, their ex–chief of police, standing up there with Miss Hunt, the music teacher, in front of the Baptist minister. She and my father laughed through the whole thing. And when it was over everybody clapped and shook their heads. The town is still buzzing with the news. Last night my father took his bride up to Cape Breton to go fishing. And I'm leaving tomorrow to go back to Vancouver. I can't wait to squeeze my little girl. I can just feel her tiny arms wrap around my neck.

Seeing as this is my last night home, Alana has talked me into going up to the Purple Hall, just to see the old place. On the way there, we walk by the Jupiter Restaurant, with the apartment upstairs where Ricky and I lived. I used to jiggle the key in that tricky lock; that was me who hauled

Ricky up those stairs. Sometimes we even hauled each other up.

The very first person I run into at the Purple Hall is Tripper O'Leery. His belly sticks farther out over his belt than I remember. As soon as I see him, I start looking for Ricky, thinking he could be over there by the bar, or just around the corner. I'm thinking this must be sheer instinct — besides, I remember, he's quit drinking. Good for him. I should be very happy.

Tripper leans back from the bar to shout in my ear, "Put on a little weight there over the years?"

Alana swats his belly with her hat. "That's what you should be asking yourself."

"Hey," I spit back at him over the music, "I thought you were supposed to be dead."

Tripper laughs. "Aw, Nancy, you should have seen them all looking at me when I walked through town. And with me not knowing I'd been dead and buried."

I just shrug, turning my back on him to order a rum and Coke.

He nudges me with his elbow. "Seen Ricky?"

"Why, is he here?" I say, foolishly looking around.

Tripper smirks and says, "No, but I'll tell him you were looking for him."

Soon I'm laughing and dancing with the people I grew up with. I'd forgotten what it feels like to be so known. I'd also forgotten how rum feels.

Then it's closing time and that's always sad, any way you look at it. The lights come on and people sort of smile at each another like they've just been caught in their underwear. Then, right when Alana and I are walking out the door, Tripper passes the bar phone to me. I'm about to hand it back to him, but instead I say hello and I hear Ricky's voice.

BECAUSE OF THE TIME CHANGE

"Nance," he says, and I can't hear any more because behind me Tripper is going on to Alana about how hungry he is.

"Ricky?" I cover my other ear with my hand.

"I can hardly hear you," he says.

"Ricky?" I say. "I...."

"You sound exactly the same," he says.

"So do you," I say. "Um, what are you doing? I mean on a Saturday night?"

"Oh, there's this little baby girl sitting on my lap right now, waiting for her Mama to come home from work," he says. "That's all."

I say, "We both have babies now, don't we, Ricky? Well, I named mine Rachel, what did you call yours?"

"April. Rena wanted April."

"That's nice, Ricky, April's nice," I shout, because by now I really can't hear myself speak. I take a deep breath and shout that my father is away and if anybody wants to drop in because this is my last night in town that's okay, and then I realize that I'm screaming all this and everybody can hear, because it's suddenly very quiet, like the whole place is hanging on every word I'm saying. I pull the phone cord farther away from the bar.

"Well, Alana's waiting for me so I guess I should go, but you know you could come by if...if...do you think you might? Never mind. I'm not making sense."

I can't tell if he has said another thing, because Tripper is hollering something about catching Super Subs before it closes.

Now that I'm in my old bed upstairs in my father's house, I'm even more relieved that Ricky didn't show up tonight. What could I have been thinking? When I look back at my years with Ricky, what I mostly remember is the pain that goes along with living with a drunk. Then I think of Elliot and how we cuddle close all night. When I told him I was thinking of flying out east with Rachel to be at my father's wedding, he said, Good for you, but don't take Rachel, go and have a real visit. I decide to call him in Vancouver, where it's only midnight. We talk for an hour about everything and I go to sleep with Elliot safely on my mind.

The doorbell wakes me up in the morning. I throw on my jeans and shirt and run downstairs. I'm a little confused to see Alana because she wasn't supposed to come until noon to drive me to the airport. She walks in and her face looks all stiff. At first I think something must have happened to Danny. She takes me by the shoulders and tells me I'd better sit down. That's when I know it's Ricky. And I'm right. She goes ahead and tells me that he's dead, just like that.

I'm thinking I must still be sleeping, because somehow this all sounds familiar, so I whisper, "What?"

"It was just so stupid," she says, swiping at her eyes with her sleeve. "It was up at Super Subs. He was stabbed to death by the owner."

Then I know I must be dreaming because I laugh. "Alana, this is a joke. Where did you hear this?"

Alana shakes her head. "Remember last night how Tripper kept saying he was so hungry? No, you didn't hear, you were on the phone with Ricky. Well, I guess Tripper went on up to Ricky's and talked him into coming out after all."

"Wait a minute, Alana," I say, thinking perhaps she's the one who's dreaming. "How do you know this?"

"Because Tripper called me early this morning from jail. I was just there. He's in for breaking and entering. Nance, Ricky is dead. I guess he's being sent to Farrel's funeral home."

My stomach starts feeling like someone's going at it with a plunger. Alana tells me more. Super Subs was closed but Tripper knew a way in through the back because he used to deliver stuff there. So Tripper went in, leaving Ricky outside to keep an eye open for trouble. I guess the owner came back through the front door to get something, and when he saw Tripper in there he grabbed a knife and started waving it around and shouting. Ricky heard this and went in to sort it all out. When the owner turned to see Ricky coming through the door, he got scared and just reacted. And ended up stabbing Ricky right through to his heart.

"They told me at the police station that the owner will get off," Alana says. "Tripper's in some bad shape."

I am running out the door. My feet are bare and I'm holding my stomach. My Ricky with a knife through to his heart. My Ricky bleeding to death on the floor of a place called Super Subs. I run behind the house to the field where I used to play and, falling on my knees, I vomit into wet red earth.

From my seat on the plane, I can no longer see the world below. I turn from the window to stare at the baby who's been waving at me from over his mother's shoulder. The funeral was yesterday. I cancelled my flight the day Ricky was killed. Then I called Elliot and told him what had happened. He said he didn't expect me to just walk away from it. I told him I wasn't about to walk away from it.

I phoned my father in Cape Breton. I expected him to say something like "I knew it was just a matter of time." In fact I was all prepared to yell at him that I would never in my life love anyone the way I loved Ricky Chase.

But I wasn't expecting to hear him sigh and say, "Too bad, he used to be a good little boxer."

I almost couldn't speak. That was the nicest thing he had ever said about Ricky. It's the sort of thing he says when someone he respects dies. "He was a great golfer," he said when the mayor went in a car crash one year.

But mostly I was surprised because I never knew Ricky was a boxer. "A little on the small side," my father said, "but quick on his feet." I learned that my father had trained him, and that if he hadn't started drinking he might have gone the whole fifteen rounds. It's funny — even when he was drinking, I never saw Ricky fight with anybody, not even a shout.

At the funeral I sat way in the back with Alana and Danny. Rena walked into the church between her brother and her mother. They sat in front of the coffin. There was a picture of Ricky on top of it, but I was too far away to see it. Beside me, Alana and Danny cried.

After the funeral, Rena came right over to where we were standing. I could tell she probably hadn't slept in three nights. It looked like she hadn't brushed her hair in that time either.

I wanted to tell her that I knew she had been good for him, but instead I said, "I'm sorry about Ricky."

She sniffed and pulled her shoulders up. "At least I have the baby. Did you know I had Ricky's baby?"

Later there was a bonfire for Ricky. Showers of sparks flew high into the sky for him. The old gang was there, getting good and drunk. They hugged me and talked about him. It was like I had never left town, the way they all acted.

"It's funny how people keep telling me they're sorry," I said to Alana. "You'd think I was the widow."

"Well, you are in a way, aren't you?"

I heard someone say they hadn't noticed Tripper O'Leery at the funeral. Nobody had a single thing to say to that. Their thoughts hung around that fire, though, as heavy as the smoke.

Through the window I saw Tripper sitting in a big stuffed chair in front of his TV. When I knocked, he lifted his hand. The door was stuck so I kicked it hard. He must have been surprised to see me because he jumped right out of his chair.

"I thought the judge let you out on bail just so you could go to the funeral," I said, pushing the door closed.

He said, "I've been at the fucking funeral for the last three fucking days."

I said to him, "Well, you don't have to go around thinking it was all your fault. If it hadn't been for me, he probably wouldn't have gone out that night, right? He probably would have stayed home and played with his baby like a good little father."

He turned away and I could see his shoulders shake. I thought I should reach out to touch him, but I stopped because I really didn't want to touch Tripper O'Leery. Anyway it didn't matter because he wheeled around. "You want to share the blame, do you? Well, you have to be the most fucking selfish person I know."

All I could do was stare at him, because I really hadn't seen all that hate coming.

"And how do you know he was coming to see you, huh? You think he couldn't stay away from your sweet pussy? You think you're that special? Listen here, Nancy McKinnon, Rena Dickson is twice the person you ever were. I know that for a fact."

"Fuck you," I said. "I only came here because I know why you went out on the marsh that day."

"Do you now?" Tripper said, like it was all a big joke. But I could tell it bugged him because of how he pulled at his beard.

"Yeah, it was like you'd already lost Ricky. And...and I came over here because I wanted you to know that I understood how you felt."

"You're so full of shit, Nancy McKinnon," Tripper said, getting up off the chair. "The only reason you're here is because you wanted to find out how much Ricky Chase loved you. How he loved you right up to the very end."

Then he went over to a bureau and picked up a bottle of rum. He poured some into a cup and handed it to me. I wrapped my hands around it like it only held hot tea.

Out the plane window I can see the sun setting. Before I left today, I phoned Elliot and he asked me how it was at the funeral, and I told him I'd tell him all about it when I got home. Then he told me that Rachel had been using her potty a lot this week, and that they couldn't wait until I got home. I told him we'd better start planning her birthday party. He said he'd heard about these great parties for kids they have at the museum, where they actually get to paint.

It's funny how quickly a place fades away once you get on a plane. It's almost like a dream, like the way it shreds into fragments the moment you wake up. Maybe Tripper was right when he said I didn't know how lucky I was to have gotten out of town. I tried to tell him that just because I now live on the next ocean doesn't mean I've erased my whole life. That's when he said that at least in my dreams I would always have a lover who was on his way to see me. I said, well, at least in his dreams he and Ricky could always be on some stupid drunk. But then he said no, in his dreams Ricky Chase would always be dying in his arms. I'm sure that's when I touched him on the shoulder, and I, Nancy McKinnon, held Tripper O'Leery while he cried all over my shirt.